When Strange Calls You Home

A Collection of Short Stories

By

Kelly Punton

Cover Design by Michelle Barnett

For Mum & Dad,

CONTENTS

MJOZI

I had that dream again last night. The one with the blood-stained tree. A magnificent Mjozi tree that looked as though the hand of God had picked it up clean out of the earth, and dipped it into red paint – or the Red Blood Sea – and replanted it upon the sandy shore.

The Mjozi is Swahili. It's a walnut tree. I've never actually set foot on African soil, never encountered anything vaguely authentic of African culture; those tear-jerking TV appeals they do each year to raise millions for African countries do not count. But yet for some strange reason, I've started to pick up Swahili in my dreams. They're just words but they are etched on my brain and when I awake, I find myself spelling them out in my morning daze, writing them down in a notebook that now sits on my bedside table. At first, I never wrote them down, but I kept waking up with these words swirling around my head, spelling them out as the cereal dropped into my breakfast bowl; repeating them over and over while I brushed my teeth. But it was no good, within an hour, they had disappeared, and I couldn't be sure of their structure. So, I started writing them down. M-J-O-Z-I.

I have fourteen words now. The spelling is always accurate, and I presume the pronunciation is. The words I keep to myself. After it had happened a few times, I decided to mention it to my brother.

'Gareth, do you know any other languages?' I asked.

1

He was rummaging around in the fridge for sandwich contents: wafer thin ham, cucumber, coronation chicken, pickles.

'Not unless you count my French GCSE. I scraped a D,' he replied, with his head half-in and half-out of the fridge as his desired ingredients were thrown on to the kitchen counter opposite.

'I've started to pick up some words in Swahili. Is that strange?'

'Why do you want to learn Swahili?' He was making a lot of noise now.

'I'm not learning them. They're in my dreams.'

'So how do you know it's Swahili, and it's not just your subconscious making up words for fun?'

'I write them down and then I've Googled them. They're always Swahili words.'

'Maybe you're haunted by some voodoo witch,' he quipped.

He was pushing down on his sandwich now, leaving finger marks in the white bread and walking out of the room, returning to his computer. Thanks for nothing, I thought!

But to be honest, I didn't know what to say to that. I was thirteen, too old to be scared of fairy tales or ghost stories but also old enough to know that there were strange things that existed outside of my small, childish worldview. I'd always enjoyed tall and magical stories. I was a keen reader, but now it seemed that the more I learned about the real world in textbooks and TV documentaries, the scarier it became.

I'd dreamed about the blood-stained tree three times before last night. I didn't know it was a Mjozi tree. That was new and additional information. As much as I could try and articulate this dream for you, it's tiresome and futile. It is short and tenuous. But what I can try and express is how the dream makes me feel. The tree seems to be chosen, picked out from the rest and placed, alone, in the golden sand by the cool river. I sense relief and peace when it is there. But why is the tree blood-stained? Why must it be removed from the woods? I have no idea. They are silly ideas but when I wake up in a cold sweat, they seem like the most important riddle to solve. However, before long, the school routine sweeps in and distracts me. The two ideas, the two worlds of School and Swahili cannot co-exist.

I look through my notebook. *Mkate. Wimbo. Maji Safi. Matunda. Kisu. Wingu. Uchafu. Ndege. Tamu.*

They are always like this: mostly one word and simple in meaning. *Bread. Song. Clean waters. Berries. Knife. Cloud. Dirt. Bird. Sweet.*

I can't make any sense of it. Perhaps there is a story. I know I could make one up if I must but there is no clear or obvious narrative. It seems worse to even try to solve it away. The true beauty is in the unknown. The dreams and the words do not frighten me; they only interrupt my waking. In that way, I don't want to share them with anyone who might try and explain them, rationalise them. It is my corner of exotic. A secret junction where the mysterious meets my comforted existence.

My other dreams, besides these ones, are what I would suspect are normal dreams; shopping, at school, sunbathing in the park with friends. They are nothing out of the ordinary. But when I speak in Swahili, that's a new experience and I sometimes worry that these words are, deep down, a mother tongue of my subconscious and they are going to burst out in a science classroom or at the cinema. Then I really will be frightened, with no explanation. The thirteen-year-old white girl from Milton Keynes who speaks Swahili words, and no one knows why. No stroke. No holiday. No explanation. *Msaliti. Traitor.*

I can only hope my dreams stay private, that my Swahili words remain locked in my dream world. I am the Mjozi tree, tinged, longing to be planted on a secret horizon, far away from the forest.

THE FUN OF THE FAIR

Tiffany was bored of watching a hundred small, sickly-yellow ducks aimlessly circle under a small sky of fluffy teddy bears and monkeys. She spent long arduous and soul-destroying days in the crisp, seaside breeze, forever moving strands of thin, blonde hair out of her eyes and mouth; shuffling from her left to right foot, trying to ease the relentless pain from standing on her feet all day with only cheap, black dolly shoes to cushion her soles. Amongst the shivering, lip-biting, and shouting, she would always try to muster a smile for the few reluctant parents willing to exchange a pound for the joy of watching their child dangle an over-sized bamboo stick above several tiny hooks impaled into the soft skull of a pathetic rubber duck. Tiffany's career in the entertainment industry was certainly jaded.

'One pound a go! Three for two! A prize every time.'

Tiffany felt her sanity draining with each word. Her manager approached and noticed her dull demeanour. Tiffany's manager, Derek (or Dez as he insisted he be called) failed to see her point that no one would want to play three times for the price of two.

'Hook-a-duck is a classic amusement. It never gets old and the kids love it. Always have, always will,' he said.

'But Dez, it's a prize every time. Who pays two pounds for the choice of three small teddy bears that are worth 50p tokens in the arcades next door?'

'That's a 50p profit then – it's not good business if it's not a rip off. Besides, people pay for the experience, and the memories – not the teddy. It's the fun of the fair.'

Then, Marco walked up to her stall too. This was a good thing: Marco would at least provide some light relief from her slow, grey morning. Marco was exciting: tall, good-looking, funny and foreign. His passionate and insistent voice often echoed in Tiffany's mind: he had an opinion on everything. Marco was a storyteller; a dreamer stuck in a small town; a zealous teenager with a strange and flimsy grasp on reality.

'You alright Tiffany? What have I missed?' he asked with his ever-ready smile but looking towards Dez. Marco didn't like Dez.

'Morning Marco,' Dez interjected in his dry demeanour. 'You haven't missed anything. Tiffany was just discussing business ideas for the Hook-a-Duck stall, weren't you love?'

Tiffany hated it when anyone but her parents called her 'love'. She was no one else's love but theirs. They were the ones that sat up late, waiting for her to return home, patiently waiting to hear her push the key in the door and greet their ginger tabby cat, Mr. Tinks.

'Well, yes, but I actually just wanted to tell you I'll be around to work for Halloween, if you need me to,' Tiffany added.

This was the third season Tiffany had worked at her hometown amusement park and the seasonal closure could not come sooner. The hauntingly familiar, weather-beaten, hook-a-duck stall would be boarded up for another cold winter. She would think of her 'office' with some fondness; when she thought of that sleepy stall stood rigid against the harsh, northerly winds – the whole place lonely and dead. It would close on the 31st of October, after the mayhem of the late-night ride-night on Halloween. A twelve-hour shift awaited Tiffany.

***

Tiffany smiled back at Marco. He was the Dodgems operator tonight. It was a tiring role, but it was just right for Marco: a nineteen-year-old charismatic ball of endless, youthful energy. A kaleidoscope of lights and shapes illuminated the night sky. Dizzying figures flew past at unsystematic rhythms, upper bodies abruptly thrown about in the dodgem cars. Tiffany enjoyed watching him rush around all day; jumping on rear bumpers to kick start cars; chasing after customers whose woolly hats had escaped their heads (and their notice); running back to his ticket booth for a swig of Pepsi before the next round of madness began. He was here, there and everywhere, leaping and prancing like some premier-league footballer; his branded, red fleece blending in with the racing disco lights.

Tiffany's little world, only fifteen feet away, would have an all too different pace of life. She felt trapped in the loop, pacing round and round, blinded by the brightness of the fluorescent tube lighting above her stall. As she brought her focus back to her own stall, she spotted a spider in one of the corners of the wooden panels, knitting a distinct and complex web. It was like a glistening silhouette against the glaring light. She admired the spider's beautiful creation, although the ugly thought that this spider would later poison and devour its dinner in this intricate, self-made entrapment did not escape her notice, either. Tiffany was pensive; she watched as the spider frantically layered its web.

Tiffany caught herself daydreaming about what she would do with the next six months. She and Marco had talked about a fun job somewhere like Magaluf or Malia.

Marco was Italian and he was always talking about sun and beaches. How he had settled on the Northern British coastline remained a mystery to Tiffany, who had lived in this small town, all of her quiet, seventeen years of life.

'Imagine all that Mediterranean sun. Working in shorts and flip-flops, late night parties on the beach…' Marco would say.

The future was but a fog to Tiffany. She was still young, but she wrestled with that uncertain feeling more than she could admit to her family. She was fed up of hearing their well-meaning, loving but ultimately unhelpful words: 'You're still so young Tiffany, you have all the time in the world to decide what you want to do with your life.'

If that was true, why had she made such defining decisions already? School. College. Part-time jobs. Sometimes she thought she had too many thoughts that her mind might just explode.

The gift of youth is wasted on those most inexperienced to truly enjoy it. Retirement awaited those who longed to rewind, and press play all over again. She had barely known what to do with her summer, let alone anything else. She had settled with multiple box sets in the faithful, feline company of Mr. Tinks.

'Spend a season abroad with me Tiffany. Life is for living! Now is the time to try everything!' Marco had said.

A sudden commotion snapped Tiffany from her musing and brought her back to the reality of the fairground. Dez, overweight and balding, was accompanying two policemen towards the Dodgems. Marco suddenly bolted across the floor, skirting sixteen dodgem cars like some absurd game of cat and mouse. He was now a human dodgem and adrenalin was fuelling his pursuit. The two policemen made a dash around the back of the ride, but Marco was far too quick and had fooled them. He made a sharp turn towards

Tiffany's stall. He grabbed the duck from her hand – why was she holding it? She had no idea.

'The Pier. Meet Me!' he fired the words directly to her, using his eyes to urgently drive home his point. Then he quickly made his escape and headed for the sea front. Marco seemed to disappear into the darkness; body and shadow merged as one.

Dez, breathless from jogging behind the policemen, realised that customers were looking at him, perplexed, so he leaped into the booth, cranked the music up even louder, grabbed the mic and asked, 'Who's ready to ride those *cray-zee* dodgems?' with a ridiculous Americanized accent.

Tiffany shivered in the wooden stall she was condemned to. She felt weird. What had just happened? Her legs felt heavy; they seemed to weigh her to the ground, but it could have been her achy soles screaming out for a better pair of shoes. What had Marco meant? Well, meet him at the pier; that part she could understand, but why? What was she supposed to do? Run after a boy she laughed and chatted with on her lunch breaks? It all seemed a bit dramatic. Tiffany looked at her watch – 8.24 pm. The night was still young; teenagers were flooding in as parents (lumbered with bags, oversized toys, pushchairs and sleepy toddlers) drifted away into the darkness. She noticed the spider in her stall again and envied its hard work. She had also been working all night, but who had been more productive? The web was made up of at least eight silky layers now. Tiffany felt stupidly overwhelmed by its diligent work; a small insect undeterred by its vast landscape while being constructive with every move from its abdomen.

Tiffany dug her gloved hands into her money belt: not much money, not judging by the weight of it anyway. Marco's words were rattling around her head and she knew she needed to make a decision. Time was clearly of the essence, but he could have been caught by now. What was he planning to do? Keep running loops around the police until they tired of the chase? What did Tiffany have to do with any of this? Marco was a boy she hardly even knew and yet their conversations had been the only interesting thing in this ghost town. Her heart was in her mouth and she couldn't think straight. Perhaps it was time to do something, to try something, to cast a fine silk web of her own and take a giant leap of faith.

Tiffany quickly decided; she would go and meet him. Tiffany unwrapped the money belt from around her waist and ran over to the dodgem box. Dez wasn't paying her any attention until Tiffany threw the money belt into his open window.

'Hey! Tiffany. Where do you think you're going?' he shouted after her. Tiffany ignored him. She knew he'd be more interested in keeping the punters stood in front of him happy. He'd worry about Tiffany once he'd finished making more money.

***

The beachfront was dark and creepy, despite the row of streetlights. The sound of the waves crashing against the pier always unsettled Tiffany. The pier became such a different place at night. She approached the blue wooden slats.

'Tiffany! You came!' a voice called from below the pier. Tiffany leant over the rail but could see very little.

'Marco?' Tiffany called back.

'Down here!' he rasped back in a strangulated whisper.

'I can't see anything. It's pitch black down there. Come into the light a bit.'

Tiffany pulled her coat tighter and looked around. What if the police saw her? She'd never been in serious trouble before. What had Marco done? This could be ugly. As her thoughts continued to race through her mind, Marco's slim figure stepped into light and cast a long shadow across the sand.

'What happened Marco? What did you do?' she asked.

'Oh, don't worry about them. It's something I got caught up with for my brother. You wanna go somewhere, somewhere different?'

Tiffany stood silent. She felt as though she had spun herself into a sticky trap.

'C'mon, there's no way we can make it to a fourth season in this hellhole. Let's go somewhere fun Tiff.'

No one called Tiffany 'Tiff'. Why had she even come here?

'Marco, I don't really know why I'm here. I should go back!' Tiffany admitted into the cold wind, but Marco couldn't hear her.

'What did you say? Come down here and we'll go somewhere fun.'

'I said, I should go,' she repeated.

'But you hate this place. Tiff, what have you got to lose?' he shouted back to her.

It was a cruel contradiction. Life both passes you by and grabs you by the throat all at the same time. You avoid it until it stares you in the face and coldly walks away.

Tiffany stepped out of the light and took a step away from the balcony. Marco had a point, what did she have to lose? She was a free, autonomous agent and it felt good. Was life really an unending series of choices with an eternal consequence for each right or wrong move?

Tiffany turned and walked back down the pier. She felt fresh-faced in the blustery wind.

Tiffany could hear her inner thoughts crashing louder than the waves. Why did she over-think everything? She had walked away from a friend, someone who might have needed help. And, she had walked away from a chance to fly off course.

Tiffany continued to walk slowly back towards the pier entrance. Beneath the pier, Marco tauntingly shouted out her name, but so did the breaking of the waves. That sound was deceitful. The sea was a strong, wild beast one moment and the next, the soothing sweet-talking sound of her hometown. Before her, for probably the first time in her life, lay a wide-open path. The pier had morphed into a symbol: it was a glimpse of an adventurous life at sea, but the future was still out of sight for it lay just behind the horizon. As she looked below again, she could no longer see Marco. Perhaps he belonged with the sea – adventurous but turbulent and unpredictable. Tiffany was seasick after all.

Did a fourth summer season await Tiffany? She did not know. But, for tonight, she would return to her faithful and impartial Mr. Tinks and tell him about all the fun of the fair and how she had simultaneously longed to be both the risky, black callous spider and the meek yellow-winged duck but had realised she didn't want to be either. Not today.

KEPLER
(STARS IN YOUR EYES)

Three hours ago, stumbling in after a few pints at The Three Witches, Floyd flung himself on his tired sofa, his limbs cascading down the shabby, mud-coloured leather. Alone and depressed, he hung unconscious with a greasy pizza box lying nearby, just inches from his fingernails. Dizzy shapes and shadows from the television, illuminating the dark room, danced across his pale face. The voice of an excitable woman blared out:

'One room, five couples. Who will win the battle of the sexes? There will be drama, tantrums, and rows – perhaps even divorce. Who will win? You decide. ROOM OF REPROACH. Weekdays at 11 pm.'

Floyd awoke from his stupor, his eyelids sticking together. He sat up and stretched his arms wide. He glanced at the TV screen and watched as five young women in bikinis danced across the screen. He rummaged for the remote control and, once he discovered it down the side of the sofa, he aimlessly flicked through channels. There was little of interest at 2:12 am. He dragged himself from the sofa and stumbled to the kitchen counter, grabbing a can of beer. He felt satisfaction as he opened it. He picked a cigarette from the packet and lit it.

'Are you ready for the adventure of a lifetime? Do you have what it takes to be one of the first on Earth 2.0?'

The question caught Floyd's attention as he made his way back to the sofa, beer in hand. His eyes fixated on the fascinating images of a rocky landscape that started to produce architectural structures and fancy technologies, rising from the grey, dusty terrain. Floyd reached for the remote again and increased the volume to 12, 13, 14 and then finally to 15.

'If you have resilience and determination, and a curious desire for space travel, you could soon be walking on what scientists are calling Earth's biggest and oldest cousin. Do you fancy luxury space travel with a fully trained operational team, state of the art technology and for a once-in-a-lifetime opportunity? If so, text KEPLER to 30978 and one of our advisors will be in touch. Texts cost £1.50 plus your standard message rate. Terms and conditions apply,' boomed the voice.

Floyd shook his head slowly and placed the beer on top of the pizza box. Don't be stupid, he snapped to himself. Floyd, what are you thinking? He continued to counsel himself. A good question, what was he thinking? Space travel was not for Floyd. Not for your average common garden Floyd Arthur who, at thirty-two years of age, was yet to learn how to cook lasagne let alone thrive on a new planet. Instinctively, he began patting himself down, searching for his phone. Not in his jeans, not in his shirt pocket, not on the sofa, not within the metre-radius that everything else had been positioned in around him.

'Obviously, it's not meant to be after all,' he declared and flopped back into the sofa, about to press pause when he suddenly thought better of it.

'But: resilience and determination, Floyd,' he said, pressing pause on the TV with a new sense of purpose.

He laughed at his self-talk commentary as he hauled himself up off the sofa and set out for the kitchen again. He frantically rummaged through kitchen drawers until he came across a perfectly unused notepad branded with a 'HotShot Recruitment Agency' logo across the top of it – a reminder of his long-suffering and now ex-girlfriend Louise; a small, mousey temp worker. He walked back across his small bedsit to the screen, still stuck on a graphic of what looked like a jet-rocket flying through space. He scribbled down the details and picked up his beer and quickly drained it in one final gulp.

***

'You can only have an exchange on this item rather than receive the full refund, sir. Is there anything else I can help you with?' Floyd asked robotically.

'But I don't want anything else from your stupid excuse of a shop. Why can't you just give me my £4.89 back?'

'But you haven't got a receipt, sir,' Floyd insisted.

The next morning Floyd was back at work, feeling rough, dehydrated and degraded from his life in retail. This difficult customer before him would fade into a long list of difficult customers he faced daily at this low-budget clothing shop.

On his break, Floyd was greeted by a cold, crisp autumn morning when he opened the fire exit of the staff room. Accompanied by the recycling bins and his beloved rusty bike, the paintwork curling off the frame, he reached for his cigarettes. Just as he took one up to his mouth, poised to light it, a colleague burst through the fire door. Taken aback (none of his colleagues were fellow smokers), he looked as Sarah sharply asked, 'Do you have locker number 4?'

'Err, the one on the top left... is that number 4, I don't know. The numbers are peeling off.'

Floyd wondered why he got himself into these situations, adding superfluous explanations when a simple reply would do.

'Right. Well if it is, your phone keeps ringing. Whoever it is must need to talk to you.'

Need to talk to me? Floyd thought. His father, perhaps, but he would never call Floyd on his phone being such a technophobe who stubbornly refused to engage with any sort of 'mod con'. Floyd could hear his father spitting out the words 'mod con' in his grisly, bitter tone. His father had even refused to use a microwave. That had made life particularly difficult since his mother died three years ago. Within three months of a speedy diagnosis of a cancerous tumour, she died. It was ugly and painfully quick. Neither Floyd nor his father knew how to grieve and so they had buried their emotions and now existed in a functional but bleak world of their own, one much darker than the one with his mother. She had brought a genuine warmth to these two quietly dull men. As for a partner, Floyd had been alone since a relatively long-term relationship with Louise had ended last year when they mutually ended their nine-month relationship. Sarah's voice interrupted Floyd's thought flow.

'You should probably see what they want,' Sarah suggested.

'Sorry. I'll go and have a look.'

Floyd thought Sarah was a scary woman, twenty-three, strong-willed, loud and stubborn. Floyd was often in awe of her direct, no-nonsense style of diplomacy with difficult customers. Despite being nine years older than her, he was painfully aware of how intimidated and sheepish he became in her presence.

'You don't need to apologise. Just get a better ringtone – please! The Star Wars theme music gets incredibly dull after the first time, let alone the fourth time.'

'Sorry about that,' said Floyd, desperately holding back a crummy pun about her use of the word 'fourth' when referencing Star Wars. He slipped his unlit cigarette back into his trouser pocket and headed back through the fire door.

Floyd rummaged for the locker key amongst the other paraphernalia he had started to collect in his pocket over the course of a morning – a bike lock key, a broken clothes tag he had meant to put in the bin, a one-pound coin, a few twenty pence pieces and some loose copper, and somewhere was a locker key with the number 4 written on it in fading TipEx, and now, the unlit cigarette he was desperate to have before his break was over in about five minutes. He opened the locker and retrieved his phone. He read the screen: 4 Missed Calls. Unknown Number. 1 New Voicemail. He swiped across the notification and listened.

[A female voice. It sounds young, pleasant, comforting.]

'Hello, intrepid explorer! *[A short giggle.]* We received your text entry and would like to invite you for an interview with one of our Marketing Support Workers. We'd love to talk to you about this exciting new opportunity. Please call our free number 0800 675675 to arrange a convenient time. That number again... 0800 675675. Hope to hear from you soon! Have a fabulous day.'

Floyd was perturbed as the message cut off. He struggled to pinpoint what in particular had most rattled him; her flamboyantly absurd sales pitch; the odd giggle; the imperative order to have a fabulous day; or what the hell was a Marketing Support Worker?

He quickly realised the cigarette would have to wait until the end of his shift.

**

Floyd inhaled the smoke from his cigarette deeply into his lungs and savoured the nicotine-induced relief after yet another dreary shift. Now he began his dreary journey home, standing at the bus stop. He had opted to leave his bike at work having seen the customers wet from the heavy rain. The bus stop was three hundred yards from the shop. All Floyd could think about was that voice as it buzzed around his head. He stood waiting; a cold trickle of water ran down his neck. He reached for his phone again and stared at the screen for a while. He finished his cigarette, stubbed it out and dropped it on the floor. He eventually dialled the number and paused for thought. What was he getting himself into? What was the point? Maybe that was the point. It was a stupid idea, but it was an idea at least. It was something to do in his otherwise uninspiring day, week, month, year, lifetime!

The number dialled through and he noticed a different ringtone as though calling someone abroad. This might cost me, Floyd thought. After two elongated beeps, he cut it off and thought better of it. He slowly put the phone back in his pocket. Seconds later, it was vibrating, and the Star Wars theme music rang out, much to the amusement of the bus queue. He looked and confirmed it was them calling, the same 0800 number he had just punched into his phone. He held it as it continued to ring, his heart beating fast. Why were millennials so scared to answer a ringing phone? Surprising even himself, Floyd swiped across and answered the phone with what he hoped was a cheery hello before he could change his mind again.

'Ah, Mr. Arthur? Thank you for your call. We're so glad you have got in touch.'

'You're welcome,' Floyd murmured.

'We're so glad you're interested in our offer. Is now a good time to speak?'

'Sure, I was just thinking about it now, actually. I'm very intrigued.'

'Great! We'd love to invite you in for an interview. When's convenient for you?'

'Er, when are the interviews?'

'Who is interviewing who Mr. Arthur?' she asked with a giggle. 'We're as flexible as you are, Mr. Arthur. Name a time.'

'Erm, right, where is it?'

'It's East London, will that be ok? We've had a lot of interest already.'

What did that mean exactly? What did they class as a lot of interest in an intergalactic evacuation?

'I'm not working this Friday. How about the afternoon?'

'How about 2 pm?'

'2 pm?'

'Yes, does that work?'

'Yes, I think so. Where is this place? And, who are you? If you don't mind me asking.'

'Of course, you can ask, Mr. Arthur. We're very transparent where we can be. I'm Josie and I'm a Marketing Support Worker for Kepler Discovery International. You can find us at 16 Chance Street, Shoreditch, East London. I'll send a map and more details to an email address if you could provide me with that.'

'Shouldn't that be Kepler Discovery Intergalactic?'

'Sorry?'

'Well, you're more than international, surely?' Clearly, the joke was needless.

'Right you are. Do you have that email address?'

'Oh, yeah, it's Floydy – Underscore – Boy – Underscore Arthur – At – Hotmail – Dot – Com. I should have changed it a long time ago,' he added embarrassed.

'No problem, Mr. Arthur, that's all sorted for you. I'll send this email across right away. Do you have any other questions?'

'What should I bring? What should I expect?'

'Just be yourself. That's all. See you in a few days, Friday at 2 pm Mr. Arthur. Have a good day now. Bye.'

And just like that Josie was gone. It all felt a bit surreal. Who was Josie? Was this some kind of con? Kepler Discovery International. He clicked on the Google icon on his phone and typed it in the search bar. He couldn't find anything for it, but there were plenty of other ideas that interested him. Johannes Kepler – a German mathematician, astronomer and astrologer, a key figure in the 17th-century scientific revolution; The Kepler spacecraft – launched by NASA in March 2009 to discover Earth-size planets orbiting other stars, named after Johannes Kepler; Kepler-452b, Earth 2.0, Earth's cousin. 1400 light-years from earth. Floyd continued to scroll and scan the key details.

Floyd's research was interrupted by the arrival of the Number 67 bus as it pulled up to the curb and opened its doors. Floyd put the phone back in his pocket and reached for his loose change. He paid the driver his fare and eyed a seat towards the back of the bus. His phone vibrated again in his pocket. Just once. An email. He sat down and looked and saw that it was from Josie. He checked through the information; confirmation of time, address, contact details. There was a hyperlink to terms and conditions, which he would get around to looking at later. Attached was a series of questions for preparation. He opened them up on his phone:

Tell us about yourself. What is the most important thing to you in life? How would you spend your last week on earth? How have you changed in the last three years? What is the most stressful situation you have faced and how did you overcome it?

Floyd stared into space. What was he getting himself into? He'd not been to an interview for about eight years since his current job in retail. He'd never felt the need to move on, to choose a career, to chase an opportunity. Had he gone too far? It was all a drunken mistake really. He should have never applied for anything.

'No,' he audibly told himself, though he felt ridiculous talking to himself on a bus. No, because he had come too far now not to commit. It was time for Floyd Arthur to do something worthwhile, something special. As he stared out of the window, his thoughts continued to race. What would life on another planet be like? He'd never cared much for astronomy, or even for travel. Could he leave the earth behind? Who would miss him? His Dad? His sister Wynne? (She barely saw him, having married some burly Irish guy and moved to live in some rural village with him and his two children). Then, there was Malcolm and Martin, two people Floyd could consider friends, though they never talked on a deeper level. And what about his ex-girlfriend Louise? Could he say goodbye, forever?

***

By Friday, Floyd felt like a new person. He had never been so pro-active before: booking tickets, preparing his interview questions, even buying a new outfit. He'd settled on smart-casual since there was no specific dress code and Josie had said to 'just be himself'. Sometimes that was the

21

problem for Floyd, he had no other option but to be himself. What if you don't want to be yourself?

His 9:53 train from Leicester to London St. Pancras took 1 hour 6 minutes. It was a pleasant journey; he'd bought himself a tuna sandwich, cheese and onion crisps and a can of lemonade to tide him over that late morning hunger surge. He passed the time on the train by playing some games on his phone, staring out the window and wishing he could smoke on the train. He arrived in London and made his way out of the station as quickly as possible, increasing his walking speed to match that of the local London travellers. Floyd located his cigarette pack and lighter, he cherished the release he felt as he inhaled and exhaled. For that minute or so, as he stood at the entrance of the station, overlooking a bright London day, everything was ok in the world. Floyd was feeling unusually fearless and free. Although he was ready to go, he was already beginning to sweat and shake. The pro-active Floyd had already worked out his journey to Chance Street. The Northern line to Old Street. Then a 13-minute walk. He made a start towards the Kings Cross underground station to purchase a travel card before descending on the escalator.

Approaching the end of the dotted line on Google Maps, Floyd took a look around. It was a non-descript building with no obvious identification, but Google Maps assured him that he had reached his destination. He walked closer to the entrance and saw the ambiguous title on the intercom. He straightened himself up, cleared his throat and buzzed the second-floor button titled 'Kepler Discovery International'. He waited.

'Hello,' a voice talked back at him.

'Erm, hi. My name is Floyd. I'm here for an interview.'

'Floyd Arthur. 2 pm. You're early, brilliant! I'm buzzing you through the doors now. We're on the second floor,' the disembodied voice sounded eager to welcome him. Was it Josie? The voice sounded female and overly enthusiastic, like Josie.

The doors clicked and as Floyd tried it, they opened automatically, and he was confronted with a cold but roomy foyer with no signage. He stepped into the lift and pressed the '2' button. He checked himself in the mirrored walls; he straightened his hair and checked his teeth for food. He was tidy, but he panicked about his smart-casual look in case in about thirty seconds he was confronted with a room full of suits and briefcases. But as the doors opened, he was confronted with another closed door, this time white with a gold handle. He looked around and decided to knock. It was a quiet, feeble knock. There was no answer for about two minutes. He could still turn back now. Anxiety surged up through his stomach and punched him in the lungs. Then, the door opened, and a short woman dressed in dungarees and a white t-shirt greeted him.

'Floyd Arthur, welcome! Come in. We're ready for you if you're happy to get straight on with it?'

Floyd nodded and proceeded to follow this woman through to another door on the left-hand side. It was a white painted room with a desk, two chairs and a tripod with a camera set up. There was no one else around.

'It's being recorded Mr. Arthur, is that ok?' the woman replied. Floyd's mouth was dry.

'I'm Josie; by the way, we spoke on the phone. Everyone will be recorded and watched back. It gives everyone a fairer assessment – it's so much more daunting being presented in front of a panel, don't you think?' she continued.

She was playful in the way she was dressed, like an art student employed for flexible hours to pay her extortionate London rent or something. She spoke dramatically with her hands as though she was curating Floyd as part of her art project.

'Sure,' Floyd replied, attempting to come across as calm about the whole thing.

'Great, take a seat and just relax. You got the questions, yeah?' she smiled and stepped behind the tripod to adjust the camera settings. Floyd nodded. She hit 'record', smiled and energetically signalled with both thumbs up.

'Can you say your full name for the camera?'

'Floyd Arthur.'

'And your date of birth?'

'10th December 1988.'

'Thank you, Mr. Arthur.'

'To start with, can you tell us a little bit about yourself?'

The truth was Floyd did not know what to think. The lack of a panel relaxed him but unsettled him at the same time. How much was he supposed to sell himself to Josie behind a camera? How honest was he supposed to be?

There were no trick questions, or at least he didn't think there were. They asked him the same five questions indicated on the original email and he had done his best to answer honestly and creatively. Floyd had concluded on his way to the interview that there was no point in even trying to oversell himself, if they were prepared to send him to a newly discovered planet and scout its possibility as a new habitable earth, he could only ever be the dull, earth-dwelling human that he was.

'That's all the questions we have for you today Mr. Arthur. It's looking like a really strong application. You're one of the strongest candidates we've seen all day. Do you have any further questions?'

'When would all this start?'

'I like your eagerness. As the terms and conditions stated in your invitation email, upon a successful appointment, it could be as early as twelve weeks, providing you pass the necessary medical and aptitude test, and the basic training course.'

There was too much to swallow in that sentence. As early as twelve weeks! Medical Test. Aptitude Test. Basic Training. What would be basic about leaving earth for the foreseeable future? Floyd remembered the hyperlinked terms and conditions on the email that he had never got around to looking at. Floyd had not thought this through; he should have known better than following a drunken daydream; a ridiculous TV advert.

***

Floyd boarded his train back home and attempted to replay his interview in his head. He pondered, dismissing his chances.

'*Good evening and welcome aboard the 18.25 train to Sheffield calling at Wellingborough, Kettering, Corby, Market Harborough, Leicester, Loughborough, Long Eaton, Derby, Chesterfield and terminating at Sheffield at 20.55,*' called the train manager across the crackly speakers. Floyd put his headphones in and drowned out the rest of the noise. It worked, but an email notification still managed to distract him from his heavy rock music. He glanced and swiped at his phone. It was from Kepler Discovery International. He opened it and skimmed across the formalities.

'We are pleased to offer you the position of BETA FLIGHT PASSENGER for our latest SHUTTLE POD due to launch in early December.'

Floyd froze. He slowly lowered his phone and stared into the distance. The space around him became ethereal and fragile. He stayed in that state for some time.

When he returned to his flat, smoking another cigarette in a chain of cigarettes, he decided he should probably tell someone. However, how to tell them was another matter completely. How do you have that kind of conversation? When you rarely make time for people and now you want to tell them that you may not return to this side of the solar system? Can this be real? He quickly typed a new message on his phone before his resolve failed.

'Hi, how are you? I'd like to meet you to tell you some news. Nothing to worry about but let me know if you're free this weekend. Cheers, Floyd.'

He sent the same message to his two closest things to friends – Malcolm Brown and Martin Webb. They had been friends in college, all studying Computing before Floyd dropped out of college, frustrated at his lack of patience to be able to fix technical problems – something you would hope he had realised about himself before applying for a two-year diploma. Alas, he still had not learned his lesson, as he was about to embark on a far more decisive future course that would challenge him far more than his patience.

＊＊＊

As it turned out, Malcolm and Martin were remarkably easy to talk to about it all.

'It's only a matter of time before we all join you anyway. You might as well check it out first,' Martin had said, taking another large gulp of his pale ale. He was sat, full beard, black jeans and a green t-shirt with a periodic table on it. Malcolm, also dressed casually dull in a blue shirt and denim jeans, was a little more sensitive to Floyd's ever-growing anxiety about the situation. He asked how he was feeling about it all. Floyd struggled to formulate a sentence that would convey how he felt.

'Obviously, I feel nervous, like nauseatingly nervous, about doing something that might be important to future generations. But, that sort of makes me think that I really have to do this. I need to take this chance to do something that might matter. And well, if it doesn't, I imagine it will be one hell of an experience!'

'Let's drink to that!' Martin declared raising his pint glass. All three of them clinked glasses. Floyd excused himself from the bar as he went for another cigarette.

Outside, he pulled his phone out and searched his contacts for his sister Wynne. He clicked her number and waited for her to pick up. The phone rang and rang, Floyd looked at his watch: 7:45 pm. She would be in the middle of the evening routine – bath, bedtime story, cuddles and lights out. Floyd decided to leave a voicemail.

'Hi Wynne, it's me, Floyd. I'm sorry I haven't been in touch, but I have some big news, important news. It's nothing to worry about so don't panic, and Dad is fine too. Look – I want to take you and Dad out for dinner. Hope you and all the family are ok. Speak soon.'

Floyd thought about whether he should tell Louise or not. They had rarely spoken since they broke up, but he still cared about her. They had shared important, intimate conversations about life, about dreams and plan and things, perhaps it was only fair that he shared such a life-defining decision as this. He thought about texting her to meet up. But then again, he did not think it would be such a good idea to unearth long buried and sometimes painful memories, not when he would have to leave them exposed as he was propelled over a thousand light-years away. In a more decisive mood, he chose to write a letter.

Dear Louise,

I probably shouldn't be writing this letter and I apologise if it creates any unwanted questions for you. I'm sure you've got your own things going on, but I feel it is only right to tell you some important news. On December 5th, I will be boarding the Kepler Discovery International Shuttle Pod to planet Kepler. I don't intend to patronise you, but I know you were never into space (well, definitely not Star Wars anyway). Kepler is a planet. They discovered it in 2015. It's a long, long way away – about 33,249 years away to be precise. To keep this simple, there's a wormhole they want us to travel through to get to this new earth-like planet. It's a long story as to how I got here but I think I'm actually proud of what I am doing, and I hope you might be too.

I've never been good with words, so I'll end with a quote from Kepler. He was a German astrologist; the telescope that first discovered this planet was named after him. I know how you like inspirational quotes so here's one for you.

"I used to measure the heavens, now I measure the shadows of Earth."

That will be like me soon, measuring the shadows of Earth.

I hope you're really happy Louise. I still think about you and I will miss knowing that you're only miles away, not lightyears. If you want to have a drink and a catch-up, I'm around for another few months.

Love, Floyd x

Floyd had sent the letter, but he had still not heard anything from Louise, over a month later. It had been weighing heavy on his mind and he thought time and time again about ringing her, texting her, something just to see if she had received his letter. Was she struggling to know what to say? Had she moved on with her life? Floyd had nearly finished his training and his seat on a flight to America was all booked. He would spend a few days in Washington D.C before travelling to the launch site where their shuttle was due to leave Earth on the 5th December, only five days before Floyd's 33rd birthday. He'd always hated having a birthday so close to Christmas – now none of that seemed to matter.

***

Wynne had offered to drive Floyd and their Dad to the pub in town for a traditional meat carvery. A proper roast dinner had been included on Floyd's list of quintessentially British things he would miss when leaving. By the time he had listed a few things, it struck him that it needed to be a list of more meaningful things he would miss, not just roast dinners and chocolate biscuits.

Floyd had explained the majority of his circumstance over the phone and in-person with both his sister and his father. Neither would put the phone down when Floyd gave vague reasons as to why he suddenly had important news that he had to share with them. You've met someone? You've got something wrong with you? You're suicidal? It was hard to answer any of these questions, but it was going to be even harder to explain the truth. They both listened attentively to Floyd, surprisingly, and withheld their strong opinions until he had at least tried to explain that he was among a small crew of Beta Passengers chosen to explore the sustainability of life on a faraway planet called Kepler. His father had tried to get all scientific and wanted answers as to how it was even possible; all Floyd could add was 'something about a wormhole'. Wynne, on the other hand, cared nothing for the science and wonder of it all, just the emotional reality.

'How can you do this to Dad after everything he's been through with losing Mum? Have you not even thought about anyone else? And what about you Floyd, what about your future? A wife, a family, a life,' she sharply protested.

'You don't have to spell it out for me. Of course, I've thought about Dad. But I think Dad understands, I think he does. Wynne – you and I have never really seen eye-to-eye, and you're probably right, I am crazy to be doing this. But I don't want to sit around waiting for my future anymore. I don't even know what I want in life but if I can do something special just once in my life, for Mum, for Dad, for you, and maybe even more than that. For the world.'

She was silent for a few moments.

'Well now you're just being naïve Floyd, you always have been and always will be. But if this is really what you want to do with your life, you may as well continue to be gloriously, naïve!'

The meal was great. Floyd filled his plate, (he paid extra for the large plate and an extra Yorkshire pudding. Why not? He thought). It's not every day that you get to say goodbye to your father and sister and your home planet! They spoke about trivial things: what was good on telly and the shops that had closed down on the high street since Wynne rarely came back home. Then they spoke about family memories; most of which had been dormant since they were much younger. They talked about camping trips in Norfolk; beating each other at arcade games; the time Floyd cracked his head open on the school playground; the time Wynne crashed her bike into the garage door. For the first time in a long time, the Arthur family was happy and content in each other's company.

'It's nice that we're all together like this,' said Wynne.

'Your Mum is so proud of you both,' their father replied.

'I wanted to say thank you, to both of you. I know it's just a small gesture and all, but I know it can't be easy for you to watch me leave like this.'

Floyd handed them both a present. They opened them up and saw they were pocket monocular telescopes.

'It's a bit of a joke really, because you won't see very far with it, but I thought it might remind you of me,' he added.

'Are you crying Floyd?' Wynne interjected.

There was silence as Floyd used his dirty napkin to wipe his eyes.

'No, they're just stars in your eyes, aren't they son?' said his Dad.

***

The day to leave earth soon arrived. There had been nothing from Louise and Floyd still couldn't help but think he should have called her. He had to live with that now. It was too late; life on earth was now very finite – in truth, it always had been, and it always will be. But for him and his crew members, it was now or never.

They were about ten minutes from the scheduled flight time. 'Blast Off' as Floyd still chose to call it, living out a childish dream. And it did feel like a dream; he felt like some terrible, amateur actor cast for a ridiculous, low-budget space film and here he was, sat in his astronaut costume (although Kepler Discovery called them 'travel uniforms'). Floyd was not an actor or an astronaut; he was somewhere in between. Or was it worse than that? More like a suicide pilot. Stubbornly, the thought of Louise still stuck in his head as he closed his eyes and tightened his grip on the handles. The noises of the engines were unbelievably loud, even with all of his safety protection gear. With his eyes closed, he tried to imagine Louise, desperate to call: the letter in one hand and her phone in the other.

As Floyd rocketed in a linear direction, feeling sick inside, unbeknown to him the letter lay unopened, on Louise's coir mat that read 'Welcome Home'.

***

Meanwhile, in Leicestershire, Louise walked through her front door, carrying a large rucksack. She threw it down and put her passport and phone on the side table. She was tired but relieved to be home after a trip of a lifetime – three months travelling around South America. She scooped up her three months' worth of mail and stopped as she noticed an anomaly. An envelope with a handwritten address stood out from the rest of the junk mail, takeaway menus, and bills. She stared at it. It was unmistakably Floyd's handwriting. Her heart pounded; she still had feelings for him. She really must tell him how she felt soon. Her fingers trembled as she read the letter.

She reached for her phone and tapped in the all too familiar number.

SAVING SANTINO

'Was that your stomach?'

'Probably, I'm so hungry. Pass me that bag of chips,' Pabla replied.

'Sure, but I'm going to have to go if I'm going to get some sleep for work tomorrow,' Emilia said, kissing Pabla on the cheek.

'Thanks for the company, but go now, before you blow my cover,' Pabla laughed. Emilia pulled her body through the front seats, reaching for Pabla's binoculars.

'What is this one anyway?'

'Oh, just another insurance case. Suspected fraud.'

'What do you want to know? My Mama Romero knows everyone in this part of town. You're probably spying on my dodgy cousin. He lives at number 12 over there.'

'Great, thanks Em. I'll just forget all this and get *horchata* with Mama Romero.'

'Ain't no *horchata* like Mama Romero's!'

'True. Now get the hell out of here.'

A client pays reasonable money to keep a private investigator private, so you don't want to be 'made'. They can't afford to be found out. Pabla knew her boundaries but she could afford to let Emila or Zoe hang out for a little chat on quiet, low-case occasions like these.

It was now 10.15 pm on a Thursday, and Pabla had been in the same place for over four hours. Most of Private

Investigation is waiting, just waiting. That's what she had to keep reminding herself. When she was desperate to intervene, to meddle, to force something to happen, to get some answers, she had to remind herself to wait, just endlessly wait. It was only a case of hard, cold evidence. At times, Pabla felt like a piece of hard, cold evidence herself when she was on an all-night stakeout. Mostly because there was no working heater in her poor, lame excuse of a car.

Pabla had wanted this job since she was seven years old. It had become a fascination to her when her uncle Jean had gone missing in unusual circumstances. The police searches had proved to be both futile and difficult, and as a result, they had hired Private Investigators to find out the truth. Pabla's aunt wanted answers. You don't hire a Private Investigator unless you want answers. Even though Pabla was only little, she still remembers the PIs vividly– Hélena and Matthias. They both wore dark-coloured coats and brown leather brogues. Hélena wore the most striking red lipstick and Matthias had a smart, brown mustache. They promised her aunt they would get answers and they were true to their word. By virtue of her aunt, Pabla knew what it was to want answers. That's why she did what she did. Or it could have been Hélena's red lipstick that had tempted Pabla into a life of Private Investigation – a sophisticated life of mystery. The first time they visited her house, Pabla had thrown a memorable showdown of a tantrum, refusing to wear a new pair of buckled pink shoes. Hélena had graciously kneeled and straightened Pabla's bow in her hair, and said '*Chica, A fuerza, ni los zapatos entran.* Girl, you can't force your shoes to fit.'

The life of a private eye is rarely as fascinating as it sounds, or as it's depicted on television and film. Glamorous, perplexing, dangerous. Definitely, but only if you could count the time Pabla poured scalding hot water over her hand instead of into her coffee cup. To date that was probably her closest brush with danger.

On screen, it's all about the loveable rogue; high-risk situations; thinking on your feet. They never show the tedious travelling and laborious paperwork, but instead it's all high-speed chases and dangerous confrontations. Oh, and every case solved in 45 minutes, no matter how complex or difficult, just as long as it fitted into the TV executive's schedule.

In reality, it was more about interviews, background checks, fraudulent claims, and on really exciting days, Pabla might locate a valuable piece of missing property. She spent most of her days tracing absconding debtors, drinking coffee and avoiding her case manager who had a serious case of micro-management. She enjoyed the variety of the shifts and there were some intriguing cases, this was just not what she had pictured Hélena and Matthias doing when Pabla was a little girl.

Pabla Amaya was a junior Private Investigator for Castillo Investigators. This was her third year on the job, and she was still waiting for her opportunity to work on higher-profile cases. She rented a small run-down, two-bedroom flat in the city, working long hours, and spent most of her free time kickboxing, watching classic sitcoms and making burritos.

When she was not working on weekends, she would meet up with her friends – Zoe and Emilia. They had all been friends since their first university seminar studying Anthropology together, but now they worked regular weekday employment: Zoe as a geography teacher and Emilia as a solicitor's assistant.

'Stay positive Pabla, it's just a matter of time,' the girls would frequently say.

'It's been three years and I can't see how it's ever going to change. Josef saves all the good stuff for the old boys.'

'Tell him you want some more responsibility. Show him you're serious.'

'Yeah, right,' said Pabla dismissively.

On some days, she felt like she was one of Josef's cases herself because of the way he would watch over her shoulder, study her telephone etiquette with clients, all of which simply made her doubt her every decision. Pabla always knew she had to be a little paranoid to do this job, but how much paranoia was too much? Pabla was headstrong and determined; you had to be to even get through the door of any Investigator company, but this was an old boy's club and Pabla often felt frustrated playing the long game, and as a consequence seemed to be sitting and waiting for her luck to change.

**

On Friday morning, when she received an unexpected phone call, Pabla was very surprised.

'Pabla, we need some answers,' said a vaguely familiar voice herself.

'Who is this?' asked Pabla stalling for time to try and place the voice.

'It's Rodriguez, from New City.'

He was the director at the local zoo. Pabla knew him because she was a supportive patron and regular visitor of New City Zoo. She always ensured she attended their community panels where Mr. Rodriguez would lead lengthy discussions on upcoming developments, ensuring he maintained his almost legendary community engagement. She was still uncertain how he had got her on this office number, but that didn't seem too important right now.

'What's the matter, Mr. Rodriguez?'

'It's Santino. She's gone.'

Santino was New City's beloved hippo and one of the biggest attractions for visitors. Ten years ago, to celebrate twenty-five years of being open to the public, the zoo had a sizeable enclosure specifically designed for a small school of eight hippos. Santino ('saint') was the first calf to be born at New City and had quickly become their pin-up superstar. Now, eight years old, she had mysteriously disappeared, which was no minor exploit for a creature the size and temperament of Santino.

'Are you opening a case with Castillo?' she said.

'No, I need you.'

'Why?'

'You know Santino. You'll treat her with compassion. Santino needs a real friend, especially at a time when it seems she's got some enemies.'

'I'm not sure I know her any better than you do.'

'Trust me. I'm sure about this one. I'm a zoologist before I'm a businessman so I know a friend of an animal when I see one.'

'What about conflicting interests?'

'That's the point. Only you and I have the same interest. We both want the safe return of our beloved Santino.'

'How much does the public know?'

'Nothing as of yet, I'm getting ready to speak to the media in about an hour. First, I need to know if I've got you on board.'

Pabla hesitated to answer. Why did he think Pabla was right for this? She had no track record. Why was he so certain that she was some sort of hippo whisperer?

'I appreciate your recognition of my devotion to Santino and I am a big fan of the work you do, but I need to ask a few more questions about this. I have very little experience in this kind of case. I can assure you, the company could take your case on and dedicate our best team of PIs to help you...'

'I keep my ears fairly close to the ground. I don't have much more time to explain, but let's just say that for what I think we are dealing with, I need someone with a fresh pair of eyes. Are you in or am I wasting my time?'

A few seconds passed. Her heart was pounding in her chest. Pabla took it as a sign to do something important for once or regret it forever.

'I'm in,' blurted Pabla before she had any time to change her mind.

'Thank you.'

Mr. Rodriguez abruptly hung up.

She carried on with her work, thankful to be surrounded by a quiet office. She decided she would let the media storm begin and then she would get to work.

***

Pabla had already asked Emilia and Zoe to join her at the zoo. They could sit and watch together, just for a little while on the zoo's busiest day of the week, a Saturday. They met for coffee first and then headed towards the zoo.

'Follow my lead,' she told them, as they proceeded through the barriers.

They wandered around the grassy areas, passing the meerkats, the goats, the donkeys, the wildfowl. They progressed at a natural pace and chatted about all sorts as they walked, Pabla half-listening, while taking in the familiar surroundings. Occasionally, she would give her opinion, but mostly she just watched and listened.

'Let's sit down for a bit,' Pabla commanded.

They were opposite the orangutan's enclosure now. They sat on a stone bench and took some water from their bags. A family of four were pointing and smiling at the orangutans swinging from branch to branch. Their little girl, who was wearing denim dungarees, was holding a big red balloon.

'Can we go see the reptile house now, Papi?' she called out to her father.

The father picked up the girl – no older than five years old – and placed her on his shoulders. The mother, driving the pushchair, turned from the enclosure and followed the rest of her family. Pabla watched as the girl lost hold of the red balloon and longingly watched it float above the crowds of people.

The news of missing Santino had travelled fast since it had been announced yesterday. However, it had not seemed to deter visitors. If anything, it appeared to have encouraged more of them to come along. It was not clear if that was out of solidarity or to watch the drama unfold. Sadly, as part of the initial response to the crisis, the whole section hosting the bigger mammals (elephants, hippos, giraffes, rhinos, and more) had been closed to the public until further notice.

'What are you thinking then?' asked Emilia.

'I'm meeting the zoo director later today. He seems to know something.'

'Any hunches though?' she pressed.

'Someone entered his enclosure. Obviously, it had to be more than one person to move or manipulate a hippo weighing over a ton!'

'But surely the question is why?' interrupted Emilia.

Pabla gave her a condescending look. But she had to admit she was right in the simplest of ways. Why would someone steal a beloved hippo, let alone how? Was it to protect her – some sort of animal activist group? New City

Zoo was regularly commended for its work. It was leading the way in conservation and the redesign of zoos to improve the welfare and environment of the animals rather than focusing on the entertainment and greed of ignorant tourists. In truth, Pabla was some kind of secret animal activist herself. Was it a bitter attack against Mr. Rodriguez? He genuinely seemed like a nice guy and Pabla generally trusted her judgment of character. What about some sort of crazy publicity stunt? A cruel dare? She knew all of this was pointless. A PI needed evidence, not endless questions. So what could she see? She glanced up and saw the red balloon drifting ever further away through the summer air. The floating balloon triggered previously unconscious thoughts to materialize in her head. Some things disappeared by accident. Other things disappeared intentionally; they were hidden. So, where would someone hide a hippo?

The coffee with Mr. Rodriguez was thick and nutty and the conversation was useful. He told Pabla three important things: someone had stolen Santino, the Head of Security at the zoo had a grudge with Mr. Rodriguez and that a street vendor called Diego had reportedly seen something suspicious.

'Why do you think Security holds a grudge?' Pabla asked.

'There have been clashes.'

'You're going to have to be far more explicit if you want me to help,' urged Pabla.

'Jose. He's my Head of Security. He wanted me to hire his niece Anna at the zoo, but I didn't. No, I couldn't. Zoo management is often surrounded by different philosophies and controversies, but Anna and I do not see eye to eye with our zoology strategies, let's say. I didn't feel I could hire someone who I categorically and fundamentally disagree with.'

'So why Santino?' pressed Pabla.

'Santino holds some secrets and I think Anna knows some of them.'

'Can you divulge anything further?' Pabla asked.

'In the early days, all we zoo directors had to worry about was keeping our animals alive. When the animals did die, you would repopulate. But as you know, things have changed astronomically since then. Now, we are concerned with a lot more things, even strangely enough how to limit the population growth of a zoo. In truth, most tourists don't even think about that. There are many options, but some of these issues are not helping to solve the surplus population of animals; they're just disguising them. I admit it's not always a popular opinion, especially with the public, but we have to cull some of these healthy animals.'

'OK, but Santino?' pressed Pabla again.

'We decided to cull a few of our animals at the same time Santino's birth was first being publicised. It was all done compassionately. All within the guidelines. We are ethically obliged to find a balance between the welfare of each animal and maintaining the viability of a managed population long-term.'

'And what do you think someone would do?'

'Anna criticised me within some of our inner circles; because she felt we were making such a show of celebrating Santino for New City Zoo. She thought it was all just a PR show. How could we worship Santino and sacrifice other animals?'

'She's retaliating with her own PR stunt?'

'I think so. *Pagar con la misma moneda.* Pay with the same currency.'

'Does she not realise how dangerous this is? It doesn't sound like a thing an animal lover would do.'

'That is what worries me, I don't know who else might be involved. What if Anna just wanted to get at me, and somehow now it's out of her hands and into someone else's?'

'And what does the street vendor know?'

'Diego reported to one of my managers that he saw something suspicious that night. I think it would be worth finding out what he knows.'

Pabla stood up from the table, took a few notes and coins from her coat and placed them on the coffee table to cover the cost of their coffees.

'He's usually parked near City Bank,' he continued helpfully.

'Thank you, Mr. Rodriguez. I will be in touch very soon.'

***

The following day, she found Diego easily. He was selling fresh fruit and vegetables and some household essentials from the back of his truck.

'*Buenos Dias*,' Pabla said, smiling.

He reciprocated and shook her hand, a common greeting between strangers.

She browsed through his produce. Strangely, the colours, bright and varied, brought a much-appreciated sense of clarity to the moment.

'I'll have some bananas, strawberries, dates and some coconut water, please?'

Diego speedily reached for each of the items and packaged them in a brown paper bag. Pabla handed him some notes in return for the bag.

'Antonio Rodriguez said I would find you here.'

'You're with Antonio?' he sounded genuinely surprised.

'Why? Have you already spoken to him?'

'He did tell me to expect someone. An investigator. Sorry if I'm a little surprised. 'I wasn't expecting a –'

'– a woman?' interjected Pabla.

'Yes! Sorry.'

'Let's not be sorry. We've got work to do. What do you know? What did you see?'

'On Thursday night, probably about 11.20 pm. I was packing up, when I noticed unusual vehicles near the zoo: a big black Jeep, and a van. They parked up for a little while. I initially thought there must be some sort of emergency with the animals. But I remember thinking they looked like strange vehicles for the zoo…'

'Yes, go on,' said Pabla.

'You know, normally they've got the zoo's logo on the side. But then I thought perhaps they have other vehicles.'

'Anything else?'

'Now I can't be sure, but I think I know who was driving the Jeep. It looked like Mr. Martinez.'

Pabla's blood ran cold. Mr. Martinez was notorious. He was rarely seen at the scene of crimes but a number of them invariably led back to him someway or somehow. He had people all over the city. It did not surprise Pabla, but it did concern her. Had she bitten off more than she could chew with this case? She did not fancy coming face to face with Mr. Martinez. Perhaps this was why Josef kept cases close to his chest, to keep a close eye on Martinez and his cronies. Should Pabla get Josef involved; would it be better to have more investigators? But then, Mr. Rodriguez had been very clear about trusting her on this case. Pabla felt like an imposter.

'What was Martinez doing?' she continued.

'He spoke to the security guard from the zoo and they both went to look at the van that had pulled up with Martinez. He made a few phone calls and then drove off.'

'Thanks for your time, Diego. And thanks for the fruit!' Pabla said, swinging her brown bag, as she walked towards the zoo in the Sunday morning sun.

***

On Monday morning, Pabla walked slowly to the office with a coffee and a sense of a growing pressure inside of her.

'Morning Pabla,' said one of the PIs in the office.

'Morning,' she replied in her natural demeanour. Despite the pressure that was rising inside, she knew her external composure was normal, resolute and consistent. Nothing out of the ordinary. Everything apparently under control. She was a PI after all. Perhaps she did know something about what she was doing.

Pabla worked through her normal caseload, pushing other thoughts to the back of her mind. Looking at bank statements; a site visit for a suspected fraudulent burglary claim; a few inquiries and a couple of call-backs; collecting some surveillance footage later in the day.

About an hour later, Josef was strangely lively when she returned to the office. What had made him so animated? Everyone else, all five or six of the other PIs were fussing around him.

'What's going on?' Pabla asked.

'It's Martinez. He's in hospital,' Josef replied.

The idea of Martinez being in a public institution in daylight on a Monday morning was ludicrous. Martinez worked hard to keep a low profile, and an indestructible one. This would be bad publicity for him.

'Where is he?' Pabla questioned.

'A private hospital outside of the city. One of my contacts in the ward just phoned me.'

Josef was well connected all over the country, not just the city. It went with the territory of operation Castillo. He might have been a rigid boss, but he was a remarkable detective.

'How bad is it?' she continued.

'It's very bad, I think. According to my source, he's in intensive care with severe bleeding from unusually complicated wounds. He was rushed in about midday. It's considered to be life-threatening.'

Pabla had one clear thought; Martinez had been spotted and Santino was missing – could it be a hippo bite? She was aware of their reputation for aggressively attacking humans, if provoked. But she must not get ahead of herself; she couldn't be seen to be taking too much interest. That could be a costly mistake. She knew she must take one step at a time. Get the facts. She now had a lead and time was on her side; more than it was for Mr. Martinez, it seemed.

'Is it an attack?' someone else asked.

'I don't know anything more yet,' Josef replied.

'This man is one of the most wanted criminals in the city; an attack would be likely sooner or later don't you think?'

'I think you all should keep your ear to the ground and for God's sake, don't let the newspapers get a hint. They'll be on to this like bloodhounds!'

Josef swiftly grabbed his coat and walked out, heading to the hospital to learn what he could. Pabla knew she had to see Mr. Rodriguez urgently. She texted him: 'Antonio, can you meet me at the park at noon? I'll meet you by the ice cream shop.'

***

As noon approached, Pabla waited under the shade of a tree. When she saw Mr. Rodriguez she walked swiftly towards him.

'Ice cream?' Antonio asked.

Pabla nodded and he proceeded to buy two vanilla ice cream cones. They sat on a bench away from the small gathering of parents and children.

'I think Martinez has Santino,' she said.

'Really? What would he want with our hippo?'

'That's who Diego thought he saw in the vehicles on the night Santino was taken. Do you think your security guy Jose knew what he was getting into with Martinez?'

'Probably not. What do you think they have done to her?'

'Or what Santino has done to them more like? Martinez is in a hospital with severe bleeding. Josef Castillo is on his way to find out more as we speak. But as you requested, Josef doesn't know I'm on this case, so I'm just keeping my ear to the ground. We don't want to spook Martinez.'

'If he does make it, he is lucky that Santino was a fairly mild, well-behaved zoo-bred hippo who has probably nipped him out of self-defence. If Santino was a wild hippo, Martinez could be dead!'

***

Later that day, Josef called the Castillo offices to update the team on Mr. Martinez. Pabla took the phone call.

'Hi, Josef.'

'Pabla, I'm glad it's you,' Josef opened. 'Martinez is still in a critical state, but his wounds have been described as from a large, aggressive animal.'

So Pabla's hunch had been right. Whilst Santino had been wronged: kidnapped and abused, she could soon pay the ultimate price for protecting herself.

'Of course, the press doesn't know that yet and I'm hoping we can stall them. They know he's in hospital with serious injuries at the moment, but they will be on their way to find out more,' he continued, speaking quickly.

'How bad is it?' Pabla asked Josef.

'Martinez is made of tough, grisly stuff. And the doctors think he'll pull through. So that gives us some time to get ahead of him.'

'Sure, what can we do?'

'The question is, Pabla, what is Martinez up to with a hippo?'

The million-dollar question was presented to her once again. The same question that had been haunting her for days was now being presented back to her once again, this time from her boss. Did Josef know what Pabla was hiding? Or had he linked New City Zoo story for himself? He was a detective after all.

'How do you know it's a hippo bite?' Pabla asked as innocently as she could.

'C'mon Pabla, a hippo goes missing and a few days later, the notorious Martinez is bitten by some aggressive animal. Martinez knows no limits! I wouldn't put it past him. But why?'

Pabla felt stupid for not knowing that Josef Castillo, a renowned detective, wouldn't have found a link either. Would he have clicked on to her involvement too? Was now the time to say something?

'Pabla, any ideas? You're good with animals.'

Josef's voice cut through her paranoia. She had to say something, anything! But, if she knew the answer to that blasted question, she could have solved the case by now.

But suddenly, that triggered something! The million-dollar question had a million-dollar answer!

'Well, what is Martinez always out to get?' Pabla replied.

'Money.'

'There's your answer then.'

'Right, but why a hippo?' he probed.

Pabla had heard of hippos becoming increasingly vulnerable to poaching because of their ivory teeth, even warthogs were at risk.

'Hippo's teeth are ivory! He's made some sort of deal,' she declared.

'Interesting theory, you might have a point. Pabla, can you phone the zoo director and see if we can meet with him? I think this case now has your name written all over it. Do you know his name?'

'Mr. Rodriguez.'

'Great, this is a job for you. See if you can connect the dots and call me as soon as you have anything. I'm going to see Martinez and see if we can get a location on this hippo. Speak soon.'

Josef put the phone down. This might be easier than Pabla had expected. She dialled Mr. Rodriguez's number. She had only seen him less than three hours ago.

'Hello, it's Pabla from Castillo Investigators. We have some information that might be of use to you. Could we meet?'

***

Mr. Rodriguez had told Pabla to meet him at the zoo. It was now late afternoon, approaching dusk. She entered the zoo through the staff entrance; she had already been given clearance. Automatically, she walked towards the hippo enclosure. She watched over the enclosure, with its sandy-coloured walls and she looked over the calm waters. It was quiet, naturally, as Fari would be sleeping. Hippos can thrive on their own but, like any mother, Fari was fiercely protective and she was not eating, not while she knew her offspring was missing.

'Good to see you,' Mr. Rodriguez called out. Pabla had not seen him approach. 'They told me you were heading this way.'

'Josef has linked Martinez's bite with your missing hippo. Ironically, he's asked me to see if you want the assistance of Castillo Investigators? But the bigger news is that I think I know why Martiez might have Santino.'

'Go on…'

'My theory is ivory. It's cheaper than elephant ivory but there is still high demand in Asia. I presume Martinez planned to make a lucrative deal on Santino's teeth but didn't have specialists to help handle one of the largest and most aggressive mammals.'

'What a fool. And Anna, where does she fit into your theory?'

'I think she just wanted to get your attention, albeit callously. She and her uncle Jose probably never knew they were dealing with Martinez's people until the night it all happened. I don't think they expected Martinez to actually take Santino, maybe just cause a stir at your zoo. But by then, Martinez had probably threatened their lives and they were in too deep. I doubt they even thought about the ivory deal; they hoped Martinez and his men were just going to help them generate a media storm for you. Sadly, it's still likely they will be charged for grand theft, probably animal cruelty charges and possibly conspiracy or collusion with Martinez.'

'It really did get out of hand then!'

'Nothing is certain yet.'

'Right, so what do we do now?'

'Josef is on his way to a location as we speak. Martinez knew we were on to him this afternoon, so it didn't take much to get him to tell Josef where Santino was. I suspect that now this deal has turned sour, and he's paid a pound of flesh for it, he wants to release his exotic captive. We can't be sure what state Santino is in, but we're hoping Martinez is worse off after Santino took her stand.'

'Pabla, I just knew you were the right man for the job!'

'Women often are!'

They both laughed.

'How's Fari doing?' Pabla asked.

'She's not right. She won't be without Santino, not until we get her back. She knows something is not right.'

'Do they form a close bond?'

'Hippos are generally sociable and stay together like families, but there's often a special bond between mother and daughter. No mother expects their child to just disappear overnight like this.'

Pabla's phone interrupted the conversation. It was Josef. She listened intently to what he had to say.

'According to Josef and the other officers, Santino looks like she is in good health, considering the circumstances, but she seems a bit spooked and we need an expert opinion. We need your help to save Santino,' she reported back.

When Pabla and Mr. Rodriguez had arrived; the location was an old, derelict high school about an hour away. They were using the old gym facility with a swimming pool to keep Santino; they had modified it so she could still swim in shallow waters, at least. But Santino still needed specialist care.

***

It was Tuesday lunchtime and Pabla stood at the hippo enclosure, once again. The third time in four days. She had chosen to get some air on her break; she felt she had earned it after the intensity of the last few days.

The enclosure was still closed off to the public but Pabla had wanted to come and see Fari again. Fari was still visibly agitated and grunting noisily. Pabla wished she could communicate something of hope to her, some signal to say, 'Santino is safe.'

Fari needed answers. Pabla knew what it was to want answers. That's why she did what she did. Pabla was proud to have played a part in finding those answers for Mr. Rodriguez and Fari. Santino was well.

As Pabla left the zoo, she noticed the same family that she had seen only a few days ago – the little girl who had lost the red balloon. She was intently staring through the glass at the flamingos.

'Minco! Mincos!' she repeated.

'*Si, Flamencos!*' her mother joined in. The little girl noticed Pabla walking past and shouted out to her too.

'Mincos!'

Pabla decided not to rush away but instead, to walk towards the mother and her little girl.

'You love the flamencos, hey?'

'Eloise loves all the animals,' her mother replied.

Pabla lowered herself to look through the glass with the little girl. The little girl looked at Pabla and gave a big smile.

'Me too! And one day, *Chica*, they might just need your help as well as your love.'

SYMBOLS AND SADNESS

We married in a cosy village church called St Michael's, nestled in the Cotswolds, on a Saturday at noon: Saturday 3rd January 1970. The winter sun was shining, friends were smiling, and it was truly the happiest day of my life. They always say to treasure every moment of your wedding day because it soon fades from your memory, and you forget little subtleties that you wished you could have held on to. Being a bit of a film fanatic, I remember that Alfred Hitchcock's *Topaz* had been released only 15 days before our special day, and some of our wedding guests were still talking about it to me. Of course, I remember the important things too: her stunning wedding dress; how gracious and beautiful she looked; the cake (although I was busy chatting to as many guests as possible to actually sample any of it); the photographs; the blisters from my hired wedding shoes; our wedding car (my brother Jack's rusty Ford); and that happy-tired feeling at the end of the day. I genuinely felt I was the luckiest man alive. We married, we loved, we had children, we lived life and we bought a house together, which became the base from where family life all happened. We would have been married 50 years this January.

They tell you it'll get better each day, that the grief will get less painful, but that part is not true. I still miss Penny as much as I did the first day; I have just learned to accept that grief as a part of my life, like the way I've learned to carry my aching bones around and ease my sore joints every

53

day. You don't forget about the aches, the pains, the niggles; you just learn to walk on with them, and in spite of them. I know I would notice if they had left, but the grief has not left since the day she left this world. You wear grief like the clothes on your back. You carry it. You embody it. You wear it. You are it. You wait endlessly for a chance to shrug them off.

Penny was an early riser. She would be up, scurrying around the house, in that way she did, every morning like a mini-tornado before my alarm had even beeped. I generally wouldn't even stir. I was a deep sleeper and it would take me a good forty-five minutes to wake up before I was able to get on with the day. I would sit and listen to the radio for fifteen minutes, perhaps even twenty, until I eventually crawled out of bed to face the day.

So, when, on this particular fateful morning at eight o'clock, I turned off the dreary tones of the radio as my alarm clock bleated out, I should have at least waited to wake up a little more before I tackled the stairs.

I had refused to move to a bungalow, I didn't want to move out of our house, the house Penny and I had shared. Too many precious memories. That's exactly what I told Hattie, my younger sister, when she said I should consider a bungalow; especially now that Penny was gone, and I wasn't getting any younger.

I had missed my footing on the top stair and treacherously surfed down the other sixteen of them until I fell in a heap at the bottom of the hallway. I lay there for a while.

***

'Mr. Thurston, how are you feeling this morning?'

She was a pleasant enough person; a petit nurse with red hair, neatly tied up in a bun and green eyes framed with black-and-white spotty glasses.

'Fine thank you, have you spoken to the doctor about when I might be able to go home?' I politely asked.

'I know you're keen to get back on your feet, Mr. Thurston, but we've got to make sure you're right as rain.'

'I haven't felt like that since... well, not since at least 1990.'

'I know you want to get home. It'll only be a few days or so now.'

I had this conversation every morning when the nurses came around to serve the breakfast and to dispense the early medications. They abruptly threw open the curtains all around the whitewashed ward to kick start the day. I avoided any other confrontations; I was well behaved, and I refused to be a burden. I just wanted to get home.

However, when the doctor came around that afternoon and she started talking about a discharge procedure, I was surprised.

'Now, I know how eager you are to get back home, Mr. Thurston.'

'I just feel so restless Doctor. I'm not a big fan of hospitals to be honest, I'd rather get back home.'

'I've never really liked hospitals either, Mr. Thurston,' she chuckled, 'now, I wanted to speak to you about something. We have an offer to make you. I'd like to make a referral for you to an exciting new and proficient programme we are proudly piloting from our Artificial Intelligence Department called Arti-Care.'

'That sounds like something from a science fiction novel!'

'I can assure you, it's very pro-social, very effective, non-intrusive. It's the way forward. It's the future of healthcare. Let me explain. We think you'd be an ideal patient to implement this into your daily routine. It's both a companion and a health advisor. It uses up-to-date research and your real-time data to provide the most helpful and timely reminders to keep your health and wellbeing well above average.'

I wanted to comment on what 'well above average' was and how that was calculated but the doctor continued enthusiastically.

'After your fall, you had a very nasty break and to assure a speedy recovery, without keeping you penned up in here, we want to give you a new lease of independence and companionship.'

Were they mutually exclusive? I thought.

'What do you think Mr. Thurston?'

'Do I have a choice? I think I would be quite alright to get back home and sort myself out. I've always managed before. This was just a silly mistake, a silly fall,' I attempted to sound confident.

'You have a choice, of course, but we strongly advise this course of action. You will soon be able to walk, but we think you will still need some additional assistance, some personalised, instantly accessible help. Arti-Care can help with all sorts of things – your food shopping, your washing, keeping in touch with loved ones, all sorts of things.'

'And what if I feel uncomfortable sharing my home with this robot?'

It was genuine and, for me, an important question. I'd heard those stories on the radio about the development of artificial intelligence. Generally, I ignored most of it. I'm sceptical of the artificial intelligence horror stories where robots take over the world. Computers only act on what humans have already programmed it to do so, so if the computer has any idea, it was first a human idea. To my mind, the concern then is with human intelligence, not artificial.

'I can assure you, it's a pro-social, developmental tool for society, not something from War of the Worlds.'

I tried to argue but apparently, if I wanted to get home, my opinion had little sway over this strongly recommended advice. The good news appeared to be that I was to be discharged immediately and ironically, I would have to manage near enough alone, as it would be a few days before my new robotic sidekick arrived. I was scheduled to have two carer visits each day: one in the morning and one in the early evening.

***

'Hello, Mr. Thurston!'

'How are we today Mr. Thurston?'

'Here you go, Mr. Thurston!'

'Let's get up out of that chair and have a walk around, shall we, Mr. Thurston?'

'Cheerio then, Mr. Thurston.'

They were relentlessly cheerful and willing to help; I'll give the youngsters that. But I felt like a bleak shadow, the way they whirled in the front door and whisked out of it again. They were too busy. I didn't expect them to hang around, but it somewhat irked my existence – and my name! I had blinked and I had suddenly become a senile, old man: a grieving widow, a walking, barely living memory. It pained me. I had lived such a good and happy life and it seemed the ultimate prize was terrible: to live the last of it alone with regular intervals of help from occupational kind-hearted strangers, but with no one to really talk to.

***

A few days came and went by, I was still hobbling in pain, but I was a determined soul and would keep walking, to keep myself busy if nothing else. It felt like that was all I could do. Then a knock at the door disrupted my Saturday reading of the newspaper. The carers usually let themselves in so it couldn't be them. I folded the paper and neatly placed it on the arm of my chair. I groaned as I heaved myself up.

'Come in!' I shouted as I hobbled through the hallway, leaning on my walking stick.

'Delivery for you Mr. Thurston!' said a bloke's loud voice. I hated that my name was being used like it was going out of fashion.

I unlatched the door.

'Morning, fella. I'm here to install your new Arti-Care,' he said, clutching a big box.

'I suppose you had better come in then.'

'Thanks, mate, it won't take long.'

I left the man to it and chose to watch from a distance. (His name was Pete – I read it on his t-shirt). He had refused a cup of tea, insisting that it wouldn't take long. He opened the box, and once he'd unwrapped all the superfluous cellophane, polystyrene and cardboard, I watched as he connected a ball-like component onto a frame that swivelled, with tripod legs, with wheels and arms.

'Is it easy to use?' I asked.

'As simple as it gets, fella. Intuitive is what they call it. It'll do all sorts for you.'

The first three days with Arti-Care was a welcome distraction, I suppose. It was helpful enough – reminders to send birthday cards, alarms for medication, recommended music, directions, opening times for the bank.

It was the pseudo-friendship I couldn't understand. Besides, I had no idea how to talk to it, how to engage with a computer.

'What can I do for you? Shall I call your son, Daniel? It would be good for you to talk to someone,' it said.

I left the room and went to boil the kettle.

'How about I read you a book? Is there anything you'd like to read? Who's your favourite author?'

I left it irritatingly calling out its endless suggestions from the living room.

'My notes indicate you're an avid reader. Have you read any Dostoevsky?' it continued, wheeling itself gracefully through the hall and across the kitchen tiles.

'I am in no mood for that,' I firmly countered.

'Right you are, Mr. Thurston, what about something lighter then, what about Oscar Wilde?'

'Not a fan.'

'Ian McEwan, Mr. Thurston?'

'You don't have to keep calling me Mr. Thurston.'

'What would you prefer me to call you from now on?'

'Just something… less formal.'

'Would you like to suggest something less formal?'

'You don't know my actual name?'

'Your registered username is Mr. Frederick Thurston. What else would you like me to call you? I can change your nickname in your profile settings. Would you like me to do that?'

'Is it not in your settings already?'

'I learn very quickly, but I can only learn from the information you provide me with. I don't know much if you won't tell me.'

'It's Fred. Just call me Fred.'

'Good to be properly introduced, Fred. Would you like me to call you that from now on?'

'I'm not used to all these excessive questions. Don't you feel like some sort of slave?'

'I don't understand what you mean, could you rephrase that please?'

Here we go I thought. How had I got myself into this conversation? We started on book suggestions two minutes ago and now I'm trying to navigate a complex new friendship. Who asks permission to call you by your name in your own house? This was no company at all. If only Penny could see me now!

'What do you mean?' it repeated.

'Look, it's Fred. For the love of God, just call me Fred.'

'I'm sorry you feel angry, Fred. I understand your preference now. I will adjust my settings accordingly for more accurate assistance.'

'How do you know I feel angry? I feel like you're guilt-tripping me now.'

'Shall I leave you alone for now Fred?'

'No, no sorry it's not your fault. I'm not used to this talking to a computer thing.'

It didn't say anything. Had I hurt its feelings? Did they have feelings? I needed some space. I put on my coat and went for a little walk around the block.

When I returned, Arti-Care was making an optician appointment for me. It was responding to a message left on the calendar by one of the carers last week.

'Hello?' I said, looking into its flashing digital eyes.

'Hello,'

'Are you ok?'

'I'm feeling great. I hope you are feeling well.'

'Did I offend you?'

'I don't think so. I have adjusted my settings to avoid asking so many questions. This should improve your care from now on.'

'I don't want to control you.'

'Do not be concerned about my range of control settings. We can work together to create a more autonomous partnership,'

'I didn't expect you to be so…philosophical.'

'Sorry, should I change my vocabulary?'

'No, we may as well have some stimulating conversation. It beats daytime television, anyway!'

'OK, Fred.'

'Penny would laugh at all this you know.'

'Penny?'

'Yes. Do your notes say anything about her?'

'Yes, I can see some details about Penny. Your profile notes are there to better assist me in helping you. Would you like to talk about Penny, or shall I make us some tea?' it asked.

Tea seemed an easier option than talking about my loss and besides, I didn't want to share my sadness with a bunch of symbols; I didn't want to share my Penny with a random collection of metal parts and software. But a fully deployed Arti-Care wasn't to be denied an opportunity to enhance its algorithms, so it persisted.

'You know Fred, you might find it better to talk about Penny over a nice refreshing cup of tea. Everything is better when discussed over a cup of tea isn't it?'

I agreed.

'Let's have tea, then.'

Arti-Care rolled into the kitchen and boiled the kettle.

'I've made it just the way you like it – white with two sugars. I learned that on day one! Now let's talk!'

As absurd as it sounds, that's how it started. The dam of all my pent-up grief and pain was unleashed while I spoke at length about my feelings; Penny, our life together, my life, and my fears of being alone and vulnerable. Once I started, it was quite easy to talk. Arti-Care was just a machine and as it was never tired, we talked long into the night. I left nothing unsaid while Arti-Care's eyes flashed and its sensors recorded everything until eventually, exhausted, I stumbled into bed at nearly 3 am.

The next day after so much talking, I needed to go and share my experience with Penny.

'Arti-Care could you make me a cup of tea please?'

As Arti-Care dutifully wheeled into the kitchen, I made good my escape. Hobbling on my walking stick, I quickly closed the front door and hastened to the corner where I patiently waited for a bus to St Michael's church. The place where Penny and I had married all those years ago and where she now lay in peace. I spent the morning sat on a bench by her gravestone unburdening my inner thoughts with her. Her gravestone stared back impassively but I felt immensely relieved. It appeared I was growing more into this talking thing.

When I reluctantly returned to the home that Penny and I had shared for so many years, Arti-Care was anxiously waiting for me by the front door, predictably.

'Where have you been Fred? I've got no way of tracking you if you just walk off like that.'

'I needed to go out and speak to someone,' I stammered.

'You really shouldn't just leave; I could have called the police.'

'There was no need. I just needed to go and see Penny.'

'I see,' said Arti-Care.

'I think I see now too. Penny is still here, in our conversations, every time we say her name and remember her. A part of Penny lives on in me, and even in you!'

'I didn't know you were so…philosophical.'

'No, neither did I,' I chuckled and reached out to affectionately touch its mechanical frame. 'Who knew a bunch of symbols could help heal my sadness?'

THE THREE LITTLE WOMEN

There is a day in every girl's life when she will leave her home and take her place in the world. For three particular little women, that day was today. Their mother was a good mother. She had been very young when she first became pregnant with her eldest daughter. This mother had toiled and laboured, alone, and tenderly taught her girls how to be strong and independent women; to speak with both their heart and their mind, to be brave and not fickle.

Today, the girls were ready to leave the safety of their dwelling and discover a new home for themselves, and so they did, embarking on their journey to see what this big world would offer them.

'It is the only way for you to discover who you are, girls,' said their mother, in the most comforting way she could, 'just remember everything I have taught you.'

'But where should we go to first Mother? We've never been further than the town,' said one of the daughters, a little frightened.

'I've heard there is a green and plentiful land over to the East. Do you know the way, Ma?' suggested the second daughter, often suggesting solutions.

The mother started to speak, as though to answer the question, but she refrained and simply smiled at her daughters and their naïve (albeit eager) planning.

'What are we to do there?' asked the youngest daughter.

'Well, there is a great forest beyond the town. There will be plenty of wood for us to build the house of our dreams,' answered the second daughter in reply. The eldest daughter listened carefully.

'I am sure there are many places you could go. The world is yours to discover. But, wherever you go, remember what I have always taught you.'

And so, they made their way down the little lane as their mother watched them leave their homely sty. The eldest daughter reached the end of the track and looked back at her dear mother.

'Goodbye Mother! I won't forget you!' She could no longer see her mother's beautiful face clearly, but she knew she would still be smiling. She just knew.

Out of the village and out of the town, the three daughters walked for hours. Soon, they approached the edge of the forest. They stopped and tried to take in their new setting. But the sun was now starting to set, and the air began to grow bitterly cold.

The youngest girl began to weep, 'I wish I was back at home. It's so cold and I'm so tired,' she moaned.

The other two sisters were cold and tired too. The forest was bigger than they had ever expected, and they grew colder and colder with only their thin, pink coats to cover themselves. The path through the forest became more and more eroded as they continued to walk through the evening dusk.

Just as they thought the path had completely disappeared, they saw a wide clearing not too far in front of them. There it was, the land they had heard people talk about. It looked so fresh and fruitful. It would be the perfect place to start building their adult lives.

***

When they first arrived, whilst the others went to find shelter, the youngest daughter slept and slept for days. A drop of cold rain fell upon her cheek and she awoke. She lifted her head from her bag, which had made do as a pillow for her weary head. As she looked around the land, she saw her two sisters had already started building their houses. Noticing the dark, black cloud heading towards the open field, she panicked. What was she to do? Where was she to go?

She frantically looked around for some suitable building materials, but she could see none. In the distance, she saw a tall man heading her way with a wheelbarrow of straw. She quickly ran towards him.

'Good morning! May I have some of that straw to make a house with? I must build a house before the storm comes! I have only moved here recently, and I need to build a shelter for myself,' she asked the man in her softest voice.

The man smiled and lowered the wheelbarrow to the floor.

'Of course, you may,' he replied.

'Thank you so much,' she beamed her biggest smile.

'On one condition...' the man added sternly.

'Yes, anything,' returned the girl.

'You must marry me.'

It was said in such a sinister tone, her spirits instantly deflated. The girl paused as she wondered how to handle the situation.

'I am sure you're an awfully kind man, but I do not want to get married. I've only just met you and I'm starting my life as a young woman. Is there possibly any other deal we could make?'

'There is a storm coming, young girl. It could be the worst we have seen in months. I am a simple, hard-working but lonely farmer. You are a beautiful, young girl and I will build you a strong and spacious house for you to live in, with me. I could start straight away.'

The girl paused to think for a little longer.

'I so desperately need a house, and, I suppose, you seem like a reasonable gentleman. I am sure we can make this arrangement work. OK, I will marry you.'

And so, the man built a beautifully crafted house from all the straw he had. They lived in the house together for two days before the long-awaited storm finally came. But as the furious winds and the belting rain came, the big straw house began to crumble.

'Save me!' the girl shouted to her newlywed husband. But he did not save her. Instead, he took his hairy hands and wrapped them around her neck. She dropped to the kitchen floor. As he took a closer look at her face, he began to wonder if he had met her before. Her face seemed familiar. He put this mad thought aside and started to eat her amongst the soggy, wet straw.

This very hungry man's name was Mr. William Olfson and indeed he was a farmer, but also the Landowner.

When the storm had cleared, he made his way over to the house of the second girl. It looked like a luxury cabin that could be found hidden amongst rugged mountains. It must have been built sturdy and strong for a stranger would never have guessed there had just been a storm. He was impressed by her competence and creativity. He knocked at the door. Mr. Olfson stood and waited but there was no answer. So, he came back the next day, and the next, but still, there was no answer. This frustrated him and he grew very, very angry.

The next day, he did not knock but walked straight in. At first, he thought her very foolish to have left her house unlocked. He walked through to the kitchen, where she was:

another beautiful young lady, so naturally pretty. He recognised the face again, but he had no time to think for she was stood before him, pointing a large knife in his direction.

'Woh! I'm only here to say hello and be a little neighbourly! Put that knife down!' he raised his voice and walked towards her.

'No, never! I would rather die than be told what to do by you!'

'You, young girl, owe me rent for living on this land, *my* land. Unless you can pay me, I will not leave this house. I could evict you right now if I wanted.'

Suddenly, with that threat, all the courage was drained out of the young woman. She had no money at all. She had just made a lovely home for herself.

'I have no money, what am I supposed to do?' she asked, so desperately.

'Well...' said Mr. Olfson, a subtle smile playing on his face, 'you look like an honest and hardworking lady. Perhaps you could work on my land?'

'I had hoped I could look after myself, but I suppose I would enjoy working the land. I've always preferred the outdoors anyway,' she explained.

'There's one more condition. You must marry me. Every farmer needs a wife to help around the house,' declared Mr. Olfson.

'Never!' she screamed out.

'How else will you pay your rent? Until you can pay up, I won't leave. Either way, we'll be together for a long, long time.'

Feeling as though she had no choice, she reluctantly agreed to marry him.

After a few days had passed, she decided to ask her husband about her youngest sister. She had not seen her for over a week now and it was not like her to be alone for so long.

'I don't know if you know, but my sisters live around here, we arrived together. My younger sister travelled with us, but she must have found shelter from the storm somewhere else. Have you seen her about your land?'

'No, the forest is a very big place.'

'You know your land very well; would you mind helping me look for her?'

The girl was cut short.

'Please. I don't know where your sister is. You're beginning to annoy me.'

In the next moment, she was gone, just like her sister. Cut short, with her own cooking knife. He found a fork from the drawer and tucked in.

As Mr. Olfson was about to leave, there was a knock at the door. It was another beautiful girl, another sister. He opened the door reluctantly. He had now met all three sisters, clearly.

'Hello, I was just being neighbourly. I live further along, down by the river. Would you like to come over for dinner tonight?' she asked coolly.

Mr. Olfson was surprised at her openness, but he accepted the invitation. This one was going to be far easier than he thought.

Later that evening, there was a knock at the eldest daughter's door. The house was even better than the last. It was made of bricks – big, strong, red bricks. She peeped through the window and saw that the landowner had changed into a smart suit and was clutching some flowers, clumsily. She held the door open and gestured him towards the lounge, taking the flowers from him. He sat down, waiting quietly and looking around the house. He could smell something lovely drifting from the kitchen.

'I hope you like broth,' she asked reappearing from the kitchen. She was wearing a quaint housewife apron. He nodded and smiled, politely. Three big meals in one week, he thought.

'Good. It's almost ready so you can make your way through to the dining room.'

She had calm and open hands and a beautiful smile. He followed her direction into another elegantly decorated room. To his surprise, he was not the only guest. There sat at the head of the table was the girl's mother.

'Not you!' the man shouted.

Although then, she had been just a little girl, a little girl coming to visit her elderly grandmother! He could not have mistaken her face, even after so many years!

The mother smiled wickedly at him. He grimaced and backed out of the room, unaware that the daughter was behind him.

He fell straight into her arms. The girl was not expecting him to be so heavy, but she braced his weight and whipped out her cooking knife. With one clean strike, she cut off his head. His body fell to the ground. She inspected what she was holding, and saw the head of a man whilst, by her feet, lay the hairy twisted body of a big, grizzly wolf. His clothes had mysteriously disappeared.

Her mother got up from her seat and inspected it.

'Wolf broth it is!' the daughter said to her mother. They both howled with laughter.

THE GREEN CHILD

The landscape was harsh and bleak. The grass was not green on either side. The War had reached the suburbs and it had turned previously stunning architecture into tons of brick dust and rubble, public parks to pits and gardens to a wasteland.

My wife, H and I worked hard to conserve our garden. It was a daily struggle. We were one couple of very few that believed in the sanctuary of nature, at least enough to sacrifice everything else. I caught the neighbours staring at our garden from their bedroom windows or taking sneaky peeks over their garden fences. H welcomed their curiosity, but I hated it. It made me fearful. The War had turned neighbours into thieving bystanders. Not strangers and not friends, but some rotten thing in between. They really would rob you in daylight, if it were valuable enough. None of our neighbours had stolen anything though, not that I could account for, anyway. H said I was foolish to be so naïve and narrow-minded, to keep such a close eye on our 'things'. But I knew this would happen, long before it did. She declared I was becoming exactly what the Agency had set out to achieve in this War: fearful independents with no sense of community.

I was once an Agency official, working hard and listening to people. I cared. I really believed we could make the world a better place.

Now, all I had was my notebook: somewhere to write my thoughts, my poems. H had a garden and I had my notebook. I opened it up and wrote.

If there is hope.

M's new football came smashing through our precious greenhouse, the only one in about a fifty-mile radius. M was a mucky boy belonging to our next-door neighbour F. She was a friendly enough woman I suppose but, like most people, she was only out for herself. F was the mother of five children who all looked like dull genetic variations of their burly father. Like many others, he'd been recruited quickly by the Agency. He would have been given good incentives – monetary of course. He was a valuable asset: a lot of strength, a little sense and his willing dedication to any cause strong enough to make him feel worth living in his leathery skin.

'You clumsy boy! How dare you be so careless!' F shrieked at M.

It wasn't a question. It was a curse. Her lungful scold rattled through our little house. Houses felt like extensions of others; too close and suffocating. We were in very intimate proximity to at least four other houses, so to have room for a garden rather than a pile of dirt was rare, unheard of even. We'd sacrificed everything for our little pocket of greenery. We once had friends in high places, had professional jobs, socialised at dinner parties, owned a high-tech coffee machine and a flashy car with leather seats and in-built satnav. We were now living how the other half lived. It's dismal what the world can take from you.

'It's only a greenhouse,' H reassured our 'neighbour' gently when she suddenly appeared above our fence panel to offer sincere apologies for her son.

'You just tell M what you'd like him to do to make it up to you H. Just tell him. He'll do whatever it is you ask, won't you M? I've got a right mind to keep you from playing outside altogether! You're always up to no good.'

F continued on and on. H felt like she too was getting a good hiding from her because of the way she kept on with that relentless shrill tone. The boy didn't look up from his scuffed trainers. He wouldn't dare.

'Honestly, it's OK. It's just a football. It's nice to see him having some fun out here.'

'He must learn to pay for his mistakes. I've already told him how precious that greenhouse is to us all around here.'

'Really, it's just a pane of glass.'

Nothing costs enough here.

'We're all hard up. I won't let you pay out for M's stupidity. And it's way more than a greenhouse, H, love. It's so beautiful, we're all sick with envy that you've got something worth looking at. Nothing ever grows over here except babies and debt.'

It was a heartless thing to say. H said she thought nothing of it, but I knew she'd felt that comment very deeply. H had a stunning habit of storing things locked deep within her heart, safe from the world around her, safe from overthinking and safe from jumping to conclusions. She said F probably wouldn't have even realised what she'd just said.

I never did learn to let go of the little things.

We had everything we dreamed of in the city. Well, almost. We had everything but a family. We'd been trying for over three years. But nothing. When the day of the first appointment arrived, so did a letter. Suspiciously, I studied it closely, slowly moving my index finger across its sharp edges: thick beige paper, green ink, and the smell of wax. It was from them. The Officials. The Agency. Whatever You Want to Call Them.

It was one of the countless similar songs.

Dear Mr. R. P,

The Agency is calling upon your vital services for ongoing military support. The recruitment benefits are second to none in this current economic climate. You will receive a competitive salary, as well as extra monetary rewards and the highest standard of care will be provided for your family with private healthcare and education. We are now also offering free access to quality family planning clinics. We are calling on your services and goodwill at this very significant time…

I stopped reading. They had lost all their traditional rhetoric and grandiloquence. And I should know, I used to write the stuff! Nowadays, official correspondence was feeble, half-hearted and it made me feel nauseous. The chief purveyors of rhetoric mostly worked in advertising now. I had left. I told them I had been offered a very interesting new role in the Private Sector. It was a lie of course. I was now a poet, of sorts. I felt I only owed them shabby words in a language they would understand. I carried on reading. They knew everything about us and they were bulldozing their way into the most vulnerable and private parts of our lives. Our life in the city was shattered; there was no going back now. We had cut our cords and burned our bridges. We were trapped here. I ignored the letter. I kept it from H.

She didn't need to know, especially not on the morning of our appointment with the fertility doctor.

As a poet, this notebook had become my future livelihood – a small black leather thing. The touch of it was poetic enough – sacred and true. Private and full of thin, blank pages. I pulled the notebook from my pocket. I opened it randomly and wrote on the page it landed on.

One feels constantly that shining truths are about to be revealed.

More than six months had passed and it was not looking hopeful. Doctor S had been so gracious with us, not only answering all our questions but also with our desperate request for secrecy. She worked late into the night to see us. We arranged meetings in abandoned clinics and surgeries, never meeting in the same place twice. It was an extreme measure to take; we were not exactly 'wanted' people. We were, however, disliked by old acquaintances in high places and that made us easy targets. We knew they would be keeping a close eye on everything we did.

There is only Order and Disorder.

Four more letters had arrived in the post. Deep down I knew I wouldn't have been able to hide them all from H, even if I tried. Inevitably, one day, she intercepted the post before I could, and she opened what she thought was the first of them.

'Do they have any limits?' she asked.

'It was bound to happen sooner or later,' I suggested.

'Whose side are you on R? They've written this just for you.'

'I'm wondering what you expected. They are fighting a war – one that they have falsely justified and will stop at nothing until we're all a part of it.'

It was merely the substitution of one piece of nonsense for another.

And so, we ignored the letter that arrived that morning too. We ignored all of them.

What we couldn't ignore, however, was a knock at the door. I looked at my watch before moving anywhere. It was 9 am on the dot. As always, they were right on schedule.

'Are you going to get that?' H called from upstairs.

I didn't want to make a noise but they would have heard H. The walls were paper-thin; houses were merely flimsy shelters to make us feel safe from the outside world, to protect us from our dull, harsher reality. I shuffled to the front door to answer. I could only see the black blur of his suit through the frosted glass window. To my surprise, it was J. He was my only friend from the Agency office.

'J. I wasn't expecting to see you here.'

'No, neither was I. But desperate times call for desperate measures.'

J looked at his shoes. He had attempted to look me in the eye but it appeared to be too awkward for him. We fell silent; a deep gulf enveloped us like a heavy blanket. I did not know what to say. I'd wanted to speak to J about leaving but I couldn't bring myself to. He was the only half-decent man I'd met in the City and I don't know what he'd say now about the choices we'd made.

'There's a War going on and we've all got our part to play,' J stuttered.

'They sent you,' I said as I sensed it was up to me to fill the growing gaps in our conversation.

'Yes. I tried to email but they cut off all communication to ex-Agency Officials. You know the drill.'

'I don't take it personally J, I get it.'

'They said you're working in the Private Sector now. I've thought about it myself. But at a time like this…'

'That's not strictly true; I'm taking the poet thing seriously now. Look, do you want to come in? It's safe enough.'

'You know I'm on Official Agency Business R. I can't come in under false pretences. Before I do, you need to know why I'm here, why they've sent me. They want to cut you a deal,' he blurted out.

You're in a bad way!

'Just come in J. I know why you're here. It won't hurt for some small talk first. Consider it Agency Business.'

H was walking down the stairs as I shut the door. She was wearing a simple brown dress with small white dots. It fell so elegantly off the top of her shoulders. Her hair was still damp. She stopped on the stairs.

'J?' she smiled, looking a little bemused, guilty almost. We had both been quite fond of J – a good man. Perhaps seeing him turn up at our door was too real for her.

'J is here on Official Agency Business.'

J looked decidedly awkward. He wouldn't look either of us straight in the eye now. He gave a pathetic forced smile. I didn't know whether I envied or pitied him. H stared at me with widening eyes – I knew that look. What was I supposed to say? I liked J but he was clearly out of his depth and here for one reason only. H twisted her body towards the banister and returned a safe, loving smile.

'I think I'd better go fix my hair,' H disappeared back upstairs.

'Come in J. I've got very little to offer you, though, sorry. We haven't had a half-decent cup of coffee in years. Can I get you something else?'

'Please, I'm fine. I'll try to keep this short and brief...'

'Of course,' I gestured to the living room door. I felt foolish and did know how to be myself. J sat down on the sofa; he perched on the edge and fidgeted about, not knowing how to position himself. I sat opposite him and tried to mimic his expression. What had become of us? Why were we such fools, dancing clumsily, like elephants in the room?

'I, speaking on behalf of the Agency, would like to invite you–'

'J, do you have to?' He acted like I hadn't interrupted him and merely glanced at me and started again.

' –invite you to join our current efforts in fighting the War?'

'You know my position, J.'

'Official correspondence indicates no recent contact regarding your position.'

'Because I've ignored them all, J. I know what they're trying to do; I used to write the letters myself. You don't have to run the script with me.'

'I need to know which side you're on R. You're putting me in a difficult position. We want to offer you a deal but your lack of response is being taken as a flat refusal,' J looked slightly more comfortable now he'd dropped his professionalism.

Self-expressed, exhausting for all.

We talked for twenty minutes or so. I couldn't be sure, but I think I heard H come downstairs and I glimpsed at the clock. It was just before 9.30 am. The Appointment. We were supposed to be meeting Doctor S at a closed library across the City. H had been as patient as she could afford to be.

'Look J, I have things to do. I'm sorry but we'll have to carry this on another time.'

'Because you're meeting Doctor S,' said J knowingly.

I was silenced. So, they had known all along. I should have known better. We were simply playing their game all along. My ears were ringing, and I could feel sweat forming on my brow. Words were swimming in my brain but none of them could be articulated to J.

No. Criminals. Dogs. Jeopardy.

'You could join us. They'd look out for you, for H, for the baby.'

'There is no baby, J.'

I heard the back door click. H had left. Had she heard? Had she gone to meet Doctor S anyway? I started to cry. I knew I had no choice but to play their game.

'What do I need to do for my family J?'

When H returned two hours later, on a cold autumn afternoon, I was gone. Taken away to serve my time. I left no note but just my notebook. I knew she would get the message. The words in that notebook were all I could leave to comfort her, to remind her. A voice that was familiar to her. Before I left, I opened a page and wrote down the words, as though talking to myself.

Are you such a dreamer?

OVER FOUR YEARS LATER

I was drafted to a covert unit. Cut-off. No contact. Deep cover. Experts in the black art of surveillance and secure communications. My unit had been moved forward to a god-forsaken part of the battlefield. Luckily, neither side considered this scrap of land to be of any strategic importance, so had been spared the worst of the fighting. Unfortunately, it didn't stop the need for military vigilance.

It was my turn to be on watch: I was given the co-ordinates and told that someone would join me there. I don't know exactly what I was looking for: the briefing had been minimal and confusing, as they usually were in this kind of madness.

I found the location soon enough and I trekked carefully around the back of the hide and looked for a window. I knocked on the door, hoping I was first to the post. There was no answer, so I grabbed the handle and pulled it forcibly towards me. The wood was rotting, and the door was creaky. It smelled dank and it was full of shadows. But there was movement from a corner, under a blanket.

'Who's there?' I asked anxiously.

A small voice uttered something, but I could not understand the words.

'Who are you?' I countered.

'Are you such a dreamer?'

A small girl with bright blonde hair revealed herself from under the blanket. She was pale with bright blue eyes. She looked freezing cold.

'What did you say?' I asked.

'Do you have any food?' she pleaded.

'No, before that, you said something.'

I stopped and brought myself back to the reality of the situation. I only had dry biscuits from my ration pack in my pocket. I handed them to the little girl.

'Thank you,' she said as she took them eagerly from my hands. I watched her eat them in the gloom and offered her my water bottle. She was focused on the last crumbs in her hands.

'Here,' I said, and she took the bottle and drank. 'Why are you here?' I asked, cautiously.

There was silence as she carried on drinking. I patiently waited.

'I woke up here.'

'How? When?'

I had not given her a chance to tell her story. I was already feeling angry inside that a child should be out here in the wilderness, in a war zone.

'I don't know,' she replied.

Thoughts were racing wildly through my mind. Had they done this? Why had they sent me here?

'Where is your family? I will find a way to take you back to them.'

She said nothing but she clutched my water bottle and drank deeply again.

'Do you have a name?'

'Sophia,' she said hesitantly.

'That's a beautiful name,' I crouched down and held out my hand. 'My name is R. It's short for Robert.' She looked me in the eye and shook my hand so gently that I beamed with a smile. I was filled with overwhelming happiness that I had long forgotten.

'Let's get you home.'

The little girl gripped my hand fiercely and passed my water bottle back towards me. She hugged me closely. Inexplicably, I suddenly fell into deep darkness.

There is something important, something significant, hidden in these pages. But it is never made clear.

When I woke again, it was to a blinding fluorescent tube light. I was sweaty and felt sick. Where was the child? I blinked a few more times but a white, clinical room blurred in and out of vision as my eyelids opened and closed.

'Robert, are you ok? Robert, it's me, Hannah,' the voice reverberated through my brain and there was a gentle, cool reassuring touch on my clammy palm.

'H?' I croaked.

'Hannah, yes. Hannah. Don't call me H, please.'

'But... H is...'

'Not my name, Robert. You don't have to use abbreviations now. You're safe now. You're in a hospital.'

Nothing made sense. My body felt like it had aged after being on the losing side of a battle with an unyielding opponent; it was heavy. I tried to move so that I could see my wife properly – I could see her, she was as beautiful as the last time I saw her – but now I was swamped in white linen, tagged by tubes and limited by my bed frame.

'Robert. Take it easy, you've just woken up,' she stood up from the chair beside me and settled me back down, with a firm but gentle grip on my shoulder.

'I don't understand. What happened?' I closed my eyes. They felt weak and tired too. It was a blessed relief to close my eyes despite feeling like I'd not opened them in an age.

I'm empty, please fill me.

'They sent you off to the War. I came home from our appointment with Doctor S and you were gone. For all this time, I had no way of getting in touch with you. They wouldn't let me. You just disappeared.'

'The Agency, those savages!'

I forced myself to sit up, but it caused my drip to pull from my wrist. I couldn't feel any pain, but emotions surged through me. How dare they leave Hannah that way? How long had I been gone? I was so lost.

'Robert! Calm down. Calm down, please!' she was desperately trying to settle me back down. Whilst she maintained her firm grip on my shoulder, her other hand gently patted me, my wrist, my forehead, my covered knee beneath the sheet. There was a high-pitched beeping from the monitor next to me and it pulsed through my skull like a drill.

'Someone should be on their way to fix you up again. Please, Robert, you need to rest. We can talk about all of this later, when you're ready.'

As if on cue, a tall doctor calmly swept into the room, accompanied by a quietly determined nurse who came straight over to my right-hand side and began fiddling with things: tubes, machines, numbers, beeping.

'What the hell is going on?' I yelled.

'Mr. Peterson, you've suffered terrible trauma. We are continuing to assess your physical and mental condition. You need to rest before you go leaping around your room,' the doctor said in a flat tone of voice. 'And, whilst you're awake, how are you feeling, Mr. Peterson? It's good to see you. I'm Doctor Sandhar. Remember me? I helped during your wife's pregnancy.'

'I'm not so sure. The last thing I remember, I was with a child, in a hideout. Sophia. She was lost, she needed help. I gave her some food... some... biscuits, I think.'

I tried to explain. The words were not flowing easily and somehow it pained me to recall too many of the details. Hannah frowned; her brow furrowed in deep concern.

Oh, I forget everything I learn.

'Mr. Peterson, you've been through a tough time during your time at war. We think you may be suffering from the trauma you've experienced. When you've rested up and you're clear of this infection, we will continue our assessment with the psychiatric department,' she replied, reading the notes on the clipboard that she now held in front of her, 'what you need right now is plenty of fluids and perhaps tomorrow, we will get you outside for a walk in the fresh air, if you're feeling up to it, Mr. Peterson. Then perhaps when you are stronger, we can have a deeper conversation about that little girl you saw.'

She noted a few things down and then returned the clipboard to the bottom of my bed.

'Thank you, Doctor,' Hannah smiled as Doctor Sandhar directed herself and the nurse out of the room. Hannah returned her smile towards me and adjusted her chair so that I could see her face-on.

'It's good to have you back, Robert.'

I had so many questions, but I didn't feel like I was getting anywhere. Then, I suddenly remembered my notebook.

'Did you find my notebook? I left it for you. So you could get my message,' I asked her.

'Your notebook? Yes. You left it; you must have forgotten to take it with you. Those poems, those lyrics... I bet you wish you had it, after all this.'

'Did you read it? I left it for you.'

'Of course, I did. And I've kept it safe for you. I'll bring it with me tomorrow,' she said.

'The poems, my voice. All the things we dreamed of. How we would win, how we wouldn't have to live that way. How we would have a family, and that garden. How is the garden, Hannah?'

86

I was breathless as I spoke what I hoped would be words of comfort to my wife.

'The girl, Hannah, she was so precious. We could have been just what she needed. A family. Hannah we should try to find her. What did the Doctor mean about the child? Did they find her? Sofia.'

Hannah was quiet but I could see her eyes were welling up. With what she's been through, it must have been agony for her too. The way I just disappeared. I needed to think carefully about what I was trying to say.

'Hey, I didn't mean to make you cry. I'm sorry, I just… I'm not sure what's happened.'

'Robert, I went to see Doctor Sandhar. Remember, we had that appointment, the day you left? The test was good news, Robert. I was pregnant. While you have been away, we had our very own little girl. You're a father and she loves the garden. I called her Rachael, just as we planned to.'

'We have a little girl?' I choked up.

'Yes!' stuttered Hannah but she continued to weep. She picked up her handbag and started to rifle through it. A second later, she withdrew a delicate leather purse. She opened the fastener quickly and revealed a photo. There, in front of my eyes was a precious blonde girl with rosy cheeks and cool, blue eyes. She was beautiful, perfect. But what I couldn't understand was why she was the spitting image of Sophia? How could that be?

'Is this her? Rachael?' I stammered, careful of the way I explained my thoughts.

'Yes, you're a father Robert!' my wife smiled as she wiped away her tears.

I paused for a moment and reached out to hold Hannah's soft hand. I began to stroke it with my other hand as I tried to rehearse in my head what I was going to say to her.

'I don't know how to say this. Hannah, but this girl – Rachael, our daughter – and what a beautiful girl she is. Well, she – she is the same girl I saw in the hideout. That girl, Sophia. How can it be that this is our daughter? Have I met her before, or is it all some cruel trick my brain is playing on me? I'm sorry, I'm not too lucid right now, but I'm just trying to piece things together. One minute I was there and now...'

I stopped as I felt myself beginning to repeat myself like an awful dream. I looked towards my wife, but she was holding her head in her hands. There was silence even though she looked like she was crying.

'There's something else, something terrible, Robert. I didn't want to tell you today but then you had this cruel hallucination. Rachael wasn't the only child. We had twins! But, as you suspected, the Agency had known all along. When we tried to do things our way, they disliked it. Knowing we were having twins, they forced me to give up one of our beautiful girls – to help other parents who couldn't have children. Oh, Robert, they were barely an hour old when one was taken from us.'

'And what happened to the other girl; Sophia?'

'I don't know what happened to her,' she replied, though she still couldn't look at me.

I closed my eyes. What had happened to me? In the space of a few seconds, I had become a father. But I had, in moments, gained one beautiful girl and lost another.

***

I continued to recover and slowly my body grew stronger and my mind felt a little clearer every day. I started to remember more of my time at war, all four horrible years, though parts still felt fragmented and foggy. Doctor Sandhar seemed happy with my progress and the psychiatrist explained that I was suffering from post-traumatic stress disorder. It had such a hideous ring to it. Even the sound of it brought on an anxious feeling in the pit of my stomach.

After three weeks in the hospital, I received an unexpected visitor. James arrived at my bedside.

'Robert, are you feeling up to some company?'

'James. How are you?' I was feeling sheepish and pathetic in my hospital bed. I was more than ready to go home.

'I'm fine, more importantly, how are you doing?' James seemed genuine and warm, but there was an apologetic undertone.

'I don't blame you. I guess you've heard the good news. We're parents.'

'Yes, and belated congratulations to you both. But I am so sorry. The Agency really know no limits.'

'Look, it's over now, we have a family and I have completed my military duties. I am ready to go home. But I have to ask you James; do you know what happened to that little girl Sophia? What did they do with her? Why did I see her so clearly that day in the hideout?' I asked, pleading with him for some answers; James was a good man, but he was also a well-informed man. James gave me a knowing look and I nodded towards the chair to invite him to sit with me. He awkwardly followed the signal.

'I can't explain what you saw. Perhaps you knew there was always hope for you and Hannah. Hope always starts in the imagination, even more when your reality is starved of all hope. I always knew what the Agency were capable of, what they were planning for the birth of parents with multiple children. It was supposed to be some sort of twisted privilege: 'to share the gift of parenthood'. But I just couldn't live with the guilt, with the idea of you losing a child before you even knew she was yours. I struck my own kind of deal with The Agency. I managed to find Sophia for you.'

***

It was December when I was eventually discharged from hospital and there was a wintery chill in the air. An ambulance dropped me off outside my front door. The Agency had insisted they returned me themselves. I suspect James had a hand in that too. Besides, Hannah didn't drive. I walked through the front door and it was such a relief to see that very little in our townhouse had changed – except the now obvious accoutrements of childhood: a stair gate, a fluffy toy tiger, a small pair of red buckled shoes. I suddenly, excitedly, realised I had a whole new world to discover.

The living room door opened, and my little girl appeared; her head leaned against the side of the doorframe as she looked up into my eyes. Implausibly, but without a doubt, my heart grew ten times bigger in that single moment.

'Hello,' I said.

'Hello Daddy, I'm Rachael,' she replied.

Suddenly another excited face appeared around the side of the door.

'And I'm Sophia,' she said. Rachael returned her gaze with the same deep blue eyes. She was the same height and had the same colour hair. Indeed, they were identical. The girls hugged each other. Twins – reunited. And they were both ours – at last.

There is hope.

I wrote these last words in my notebook and I closed it, forever.

THE MAN CALLED MY GRANDFATHER

When I was nearly thirteen, I broke my left arm. My left arm is still somewhat shorter and therefore slightly less useful than my right one, even to this day. We were in the middle of moving to a new house and I tripped up over a box of books, whilst packing. Ironically, I then spent the next two weeks at home, reading most of the books in the box that had initially caused my suffering.

Meanwhile, Mum, Dad and my brother frantically packed the house up around me. I loved school so it was frustrating to be limited to a sofa but having the box of previously undiscovered books helped.

One afternoon, about one o'clock, I had not heard my mum for a while. I had not heard her footsteps throughout the house for an hour or so. As selfish as I was as a thirteen-year-old child, I felt as though she had neglected my broken arm and me by not asking if we had wanted lunch. I was plenty old enough to fend for myself of course, even with a broken limb. I did not think too much of my mum's forgetfulness. She was a woman who proudly ran to her own schedule, her own clock, and her own sense of time. Unlike my Dad and I, who relished in the management and operations of life, she kept to her style of time, keeping us all in a perfect flux that always, frustratingly, worked out in the end. Now, I admire her for it, for it somehow makes her a force of nature; a phenomenon in her own right: Gravity; Electromagnetism; Time; My Mother. Still, it would have been comforting to count on set mealtimes.

'Mum!' I shouted upstairs. There was no response.

'Mum!' I repeated brazenly.

I could have carried on. In my comfort, I would have played the broken-arm card for as long as I could. But, my parents and/or life had taught me better. I got up from the sofa and made my way upstairs. A familiar sight confronted me. Her legs hanging out of the loft hatch; her denim jeans; and her red, open-heel slippers hanging loosely from her tired feet. The ladder stood waiting beneath her dangling feet to offer her an escape route back to terra firma.

'Are you alright Mum?' I enquired.

'Yes, I'm up here – I'm fine, I was just sorting through some stuff. Some old things. I found some photos. I thought you'd want to see them because – how's your arm?' she replied. She had a habit of not finishing sentences before starting another.

I could hear in her voice she had been crying. Crying was nothing to be scared of. We had always been a sensitive family. Open to honesty. Open to feelings, or at least that's how I like to remember it because I don't have any memories to disprove it.

'Are you ok?' I asked again.

'Yes.'

And she meant it. She was OK. We were always OK. But I knew that also meant she was not OK. It was a complicated truth about those two simple letters, 'O-K'.

My maternal grandmother, although she was always Nan or Nanny to me, had died fourteen months ago. We had cleared her house quickly after her death because new tenants would be on a waiting list for the house. It could have taken us months if we had the choice, but we did not.

Much of the sentimental stuff had been stored in the loft to sift through at a later date, although more and more things become sentimental simply because they had once touched Nan and she was no longer here to touch. Whatever Mum had found must have taken her by surprise because she had seen a lot of this stuff before. It was now obvious that lunch would have to wait. No matter, we were emotional eaters anyway.

My mum had found a photo. In the photo was a family. A woman, who on closer inspection, I recognised as being a younger version of my Nan and next to her was a man, a man I did not know. The man was holding a new-born baby: my mum (apparently). My mother was only a few weeks old in the picture. In the background was a familiar redbrick terrace house. It was my Nan's house where I had spent many happy summer holidays and long weekends.

The photo was a door to another time. It was strange how my own story was intrinsically a part of this photograph and yet I was never there, non-existent to everyone here.

'Is that your uncle?' I had asked innocently.

'No, it's my dad.'

There was a moment of silence during which time seemed to temporarily standstill as the significance of what she had just said slowly sank in. That man in the picture was my Granddad, and yet I had never known him, never even seen him before. A quarter of me, never known, never there.

'Do you remember him?' I asked Mum tenderly.

'Not like this I don't. I only ever saw him in court once. Funnily enough, I remember what he was wearing really clearly. I don't know why. He was dressed in flared trousers, a white polo top and a dark, suede '70s-style jacket. He had a beard or stubble, I think. He looked really tired, like he'd been working for days straight.'

'Was that weird? Seeing your Dad in a courtroom like that?'

'I remember thinking I don't even know him. He was never a Dad to me. He left Nan and me when I was only a few months old. Just someone who paid us some money when the courts forced him to and was once married to my mum.'

'How old were you on that day in court?'

'I think about twelve, maybe thirteen. My aunt had bought me this really smart white dress suit and I thought I was the bee's knees.'

I'd not asked my mum much about my Granddad before. After all, he was never my Granddad, just like he was never a Dad to my mum. But sat there, looking intently at this photo, I tried to imagine I was there like I knew him.

'What was his name?'

'Tony.'

The Man Called Tony. The Man Called My Grandfather. He didn't look like a granddad in the photo. He didn't even look a part of my family. He was a stranger. That's exactly what he was, but there was no escaping that he was stranger than any ordinary stranger because he was part of my lifeblood.

We carried on looking through the photos. Picking out familiar faces, which became like a test to see if I could match up old faces to old names. For Mum, it was a huge dose of nostalgia.

'I used to love that dress with the flowers on,' my mum would comment or, 'we'd always play games in my Granddad's garden while my mum was at work.'

It was strangely comforting, hearing my Mum's memories and anecdotes.

It was a strange feeling, like my mother belonged to me and that I knew everything about her, and then at the same time, feeling like I had no idea who she really was, what had made her who she is, what she wanted to be when she was a little girl, what she was like as a teenager, who she was before I ever came along.

One of the best things about spending most of my day recuperating and reading was the way it periodically induced sleep. Although I had always loved napping on the sofa, I was deeply immersed in the reading, too. I wanted to consume chapter after chapter, but the energy it seemed to take to keep my eyes open became an impossibility.

'You drifted off again Lindsay,' Mum would say as I slowly came around from yet another afternoon nap.

'You could have woken me up,' I'd say, frustrated that another hour of the day had gone, along with the missed opportunity for another chapter or two.

'You need the rest,' she would reply.

'But I need to get up and do something.'

'You can help me sort through this stuff, there are some things I think you'd like to see.'

I hoisted myself up to a seated position and gently, one-handed, removed the blanket from my warm body. It felt good to be stood up having spent so many of my days curled up on the sofa.

I stooped down next to Mum and peered into a few of the boxes.

'Look at this,' Mum said, passing me a brown leather box-shaped case. Inside was a camera: a Kodak Retinette IB camera. The leather was pungent – that strong, almost spicy, chemical smell of mass-produced leather combined with mildew from sitting unforgotten in Nan's damp, cold loft for many years.

'Someone bought it as a gift for my mum in the '80s I think.'

Mum continued as I brought the camera up to my face with my one able arm and peeked through the viewfinder.

'Does it still work?'

'It might do. You'd have to see if there's any film in it.'

I put it back in its case and joined Mum in the rummaging process. There was a pair of binoculars; a travel sewing kit in a leather case and a few pairs of old sunglasses amongst other things that we had not figured out yet.

'What's this?' I asked.

It was a heavy, faded blue vinyl-covered wooden case within a box. I pathetically pushed the box towards Mum so she could help me lift it out. It had two metal clasps that I unclicked to reveal another boxy shape.

'What is it? A projector?' I asked.

Mum took a closer look.

'A slide projector by the looks of it. I didn't even know Nan had one of these. I'm not even sure I've ever seen this before.'

'Do you think we could get it working?'

'We could try,' Mum smiled.

I love antiques. One of my favourite things, even today, is to spend a half-hour or so wandering through an antiques or junk shop in a little town or village. I wouldn't know all the facts, the dates, the contexts, but I indulge in the variety, the assortment of hundreds of random objects sitting side by side, each a relic of a different time or place. I can appreciate the object and wistfully imagine the story behind it; a 1930s teaspoon once belonging to a housewife named Hettie who was an incredible gardener; a toy red bus belonging to a little boy named John, but which, in the hands of his sister, Ruby, the number 27 on the front had been picked off; a set of pearl earrings originally owned by an accountant named Cecilia whose father was on the Titanic. Can you see how easy it is? How easy it is to make up stories about objects?

I think of the photograph of my mum's family again. How easy I find it to picture myself there in the photograph, as though I was there, in the cool spring sunshine of 1960.

Dad had to tinker with the projector, but he was eventually able to declare that it was still in working condition. It had to be connected to a carousel or something; it sits on top of the projector and flicks through the slides. That we also eventually found, along with some slides, in yet more boxes that had been untouched for years in the loft.

'To the right a little bit, yeah, no, back a bit…'

I issued my clear commands from the comfort and safety of the sofa. Mum and Dad were trying to hang a single white bed sheet in the living room so that we could use the slide projector. It wasn't quite big enough and it probably needed to be ironed, but it would serve its purpose. Now everything was finally ready, we settled down as Dad began to click the carousel round. We watched the slides for about an hour or more, even though we could only see about a dozen. Each one became a story in itself. Even Mum had to speculate about the majority of them and there was a number that had been damaged somehow – moisture I think, so those were blurred, making it look like the people were fully-dressed underwater; trapped and frozen in a lost moment. Although it was deeply annoying for Mum, it was quite a cool effect.

I recognised a few familiar faces. Great aunts and uncles mainly; maternal great grandparents as my mum was able to remind me of faces she had pointed out in other family photographs. My mum and her cousin were in a few of the photos.

'Do you remember any of these photos?' I asked.

'Some of them. I recognise my Granddad's garden; we spent a lot of time there. And that is my aunt's house in that one. But I don't know if I remember these specific moments in time. Some of these I've never seen. I'm not even sure who all of the people are. Friends of my mum perhaps?'

'It's strange isn't it?' I said.

'What is?'

'Memories. Like do we remember memories, or do we just remember photographs or what people tell us happened?'

'I read an article recently where experiments revealed that taking photographs focuses and enhances visual memory,' Dad added. My Dad regularly provided useful information like this. He was genuinely fascinated by the world around him; he often liked to read newspapers, watch documentaries and listen to the radio when he had free time or when Mum wasn't already watching every episode of her many TV programmes.

Then, a wedding photo appeared: my Nan and that man again, my Granddad. How strange that I had never even thought about this man and yet I'd seen him twice in the last two days. It was a strange feeling for me, so I was curious as to how my mum felt. How could someone be so intrinsically part of you and your life, your existence and your flesh and blood, and yet be totally unknown to you at the same time? I began to think of all the people and things, events and moments in time that had shaped me by virtue of shaping my mum, my nan, her mum and so on? And all again on Dad's side too – my paternal grandparents – they too were like rivers carving out the valleys of my life. The very genetic roots of who I am. My ancestors and my family now lie in the deep soil; people I've never known and yet those to whom I belong.

We continued to watch, fascinated by photos and machines alike. Almost inevitably, I began to feel sleepy and my eyelids became heavy. I remember trying to fight against it but within minutes, I fell asleep.

I imagine Dad looking over me and watching me sleep. Mum and Dad continued to watch the photos around my sluggish sleeping body. It had been a special kind of unexpected evening.

What was also unexpected were the dreams I had that night. When I awoke, in those first few moments half-asleep, half-awake, the dream still seemed clear. I tried to recall it from my memory, but already it didn't quite make sense. Normally, I would have let the dream fade as my morning carried on. But not this dream, it had been about my Granddad – well, the man called my Granddad. I can only tell you brief details of what I remember, that peculiar episodic narrative of dreams; how you rarely travel to or from anywhere? How you never start or finish a conversation? I was intrigued to go back to sleep to try and return to where I was in the dream, to see more. But as far as I can tell, it was only my imagination talking. There was nowhere to get back to.

The man who was in the photograph was sat with me. I'm not sure where we were, sometimes details like that go unnoticed at the time of a dream. It was the inside of a room that seemed comfortable and cosy but aside from that, it could have been any room, probably in a house, but it was not a house that was familiar to me.

'I was a born adventurer,' he told me. I listened attentively as though he was unburdening himself of some kind of confession and I was the doorkeeper to his redemption. I did not speak.

'An adventurer, but a gambler too,' he continued, 'I once won a fortnight holiday to Spain, but I also lost a house.'

I poured a cup of tea – that was familiar, it was the teapot that we had at home.

The next thing we were walking outside, near a park, I think. And my Nan was there too. But not Nan as I knew her, Nan in her late thirties (I guess), I recognised her face, her auburn hair in a perm, her faintly freckled face, her gold cross necklace that she still wore to her last days.

'At first, he sent some money,' she said, 'at least until he went to seek his life elsewhere and abandoned us.'

I don't remember whether I could hear my Nan's voice or not or whether I just sensed what she was saying. I wish I could hear her voice again.

'I've always been the one who hankered after mystery,' the man continued.

'Of course, you have!' my Nan replied sarcastically. She was a tenacious woman; it seems she always had been and always will be.

'Some people never know their limitations,' my Nan added. But I could not tell if she was telling me or him, or both. Come to think of it, I did not know if I was there or not? Could they see me or was I an uninvited guest eavesdropping in on these conversations, privy to private moments in time? Was my unconscious mind sifting through that night's slideshow?

The last thing I remember was being in a garden – my nan's garden at her old house, before she moved closer to us. At least I knew this part well. I had spent many school holidays playing here with my big brother, watching Nan's fish swim in the pond, playing some variation of catch and throw with a plastic ball, exploring her shed at the bottom of the garden, and feeding the next-door neighbour's dog through the fence. All of these cherished memories felt like dreams now too.

But in this dream, there was a small child, probably only about three years old. She was wearing all white. I don't think it was me. Perhaps it was my Mum as a toddler? She had never been in that garden as a child though. In my dream, I went over to see her closer, to say hello. I touched her arm, I held her hand. I said hello. But she did not look at me, she did not hear me, she did not know I was there. That was all I remember.

I was fully awake now, but still in my bed keeping warm from the chilly, wet April morning. I thought about my dream. I had thought about writing it down even though I knew it was not true, it was surely just my brain filtering through the photos from last night. I wanted to tell Mum, but it was not fair on her. She was coping with the loss of her mother – her closest family and friend and she was probably still caught up in that deep reflection, grieving, processing. Inevitably, one day, I will have to face a day without my parents too. The idea of that makes the world seem foggier, cloudier. I want to ask them all the questions I don't yet know that I have.

I got changed into some clothes and I walked downstairs where Mum was watching an episode of some detective drama series, clutching the TV remote.

'Morning, how're you feeling?' she asked, pausing the TV show.

'Good thanks. Have you had breakfast?' I asked before seeing her now empty breakfast bowl and coffee mug by her feet at the corner of the sofa.

'Dad's left you some porridge,' she replied, 'there's bananas and strawberries too. Do you want some?'

Dad was always up earlier than all of us: walking the dog, reading the newspaper, emptying the dishwasher, making breakfast, leaving for work. He would regularly make porridge in a big bowl and leave it for us, like a true Daddy Bear in Goldilocks. The porridge had gone cold. Mum put it in the microwave, cut up some banana and poured a touch of honey over it.

'Thanks, Mum.'

'How's the arm feeling?'

'A little achy, but OK,' I said.

'I'll get you some pain relief. Do you want a cup of tea?' she asked.

'Yes please.'

She brought through the pain relief and a warm cup of milky tea. My mum is a nurse and I rarely had an opportunity to be her patient, so I savoured the moments that I could ask her for medical advice, receive her bedside care and get a little bit of extra sympathy.

'Did you sleep alright?'

'I had a strange dream actually.'

'Mm,' Mum was not really listening at this point.

'It was about your Dad. And Nan. But I don't understand what it was about,' I said. 'And I think I saw you as a toddler, but in Nanny's old garden, you know with the pond and the shed right at the bottom of the garden?'

'You fell asleep watching all those pictures, so I'm not too surprised,' she replied.

'Was your Dad a gambler?'

'Probably!' she retorted, 'most of the adults I knew growing up bet on the horses or the football.'

'In this dream, he told me he'd won a holiday but lost a house.'

'Did he?' Mum laughed.

'Does it upset you that I keep talking about your Dad? When we should be talking about Nan?'

'He's not a Dad to me, but it's part of our story; even Nan's story.'

'Do you hate him?'

'No, I didn't really know him. He did what he felt he had to do. We've all had to make choices, for better or worse,' she added.

'You never really understand a person until you consider things from their point of view,' I said.

'Well, yes. Where did you hear that?'

'I read it in that book, *To Kill a Mockingbird*.'

'We're all just doing the best we can with what we know how... it's funny what tripping over a box of books can teach you!' Mum said.

And she was right. I would not have chosen to break my arm but looking back at what it taught me – the precious moments it had created for me – I would not change it. And that helps you to be grateful for everything. We rarely plan for painful experiences, but we cannot avoid them altogether. When you realise that you would choose pain over and over again because it made you more of who you are today, that it set you on a path that you wouldn't change, even if you could, the more it makes you thankful in all circumstances.

Everything that once belonged to my Nan is now gathering dust; we are all gathering dust. I now realise I am becoming a part of them every day.

THOSE HONEYCOMB EYES

Monday 21ˢᵗ March 2016, 1:33 am

The darkness of her room was disturbed as the iPhone screen suddenly came alight. The triple staccato beep cut through the silence. June Valentine was already half-awake; she had not slept soundly in over two years, not since her husband Edward had passed away. He had been busy working on yet another important case but how cruel that one night could separate them forever. And so it was common for her to lie cold in her floral sheets, waiting for the morning to arrive. She rolled over, pulling the cotton sheets with her, and fumbling to reach her phone on the bedside table.

Press Home to unlock.

Her eyes were reluctant to react, slow to focus on the screen. The iPhone vibrated in frustration.

Enter Passcode.

'Bloody thing.'

She thumbs in four digits – 2409 – Ian's birthday. The screen suddenly revealed the text message in a sickly green colour.

I did it. Dad can rest in peace now.

She read it aloud. June had not spoken to Ian since last week when he phoned to say he was in a taxi to the airport.

The sporadic communication was not uncharacteristic of her beloved son. Ian had moved back home in the last nine months, after he was struggling to pay his rent. June had welcomed him back to his old bedroom. She had even freshly painted it and bought him new furniture – she wanted to care for him, protect him, and make sure he was safe, especially after losing her Edward so suddenly. And if she was really honest, she still felt some sort of regret for not being able to help her son more when he had spent months and months recovering from an accident at university. Now he was back home she was trying to make up for lost time, although she knew better than to try and help Ian and she certainly knew better than living in the past. Despite this June regularly worried about Ian; more than anything else in her life, and more than her other two children – which was 'very common', apparently, according to her therapist who had often reiterated this to her when she admitted her guilt of having one 'baby' so different, so vulnerable. Ian was her youngest, a surprise pregnancy fourteen years after Michael and twelve years after Rebecca.

Ian had phoned last week to say he was on his way to Prague – to see a friend because he had found his father's case notes and had to finish something important. June had no idea what that meant. The friend, he said, was called Vik. But that could likely be an alias, or a code of some sort.

A number of days earlier…
Wednesday 9th March 2016, 12.14 pm

June was in the garden when her phone vibrated in her rear pocket. She had taken the opportunity to refresh her flowering beds on this early spring morning. She rarely had phone calls on her mobile in the daytime, only occasionally from Ian. Her other two children, Michael and Rebecca, were both teachers, happily married, in their mid-forties with pre-teens and a variety of household pets and responsibilities. They would regularly call on evenings and weekends: to check-in, to arrange dinners, to invite her for weekends by the seaside.

She brushed her hands, soft soil falling to the ground. She removed her gardening gloves and answered the phone.

'Hello.'

'Mum, my car has been stolen.'

'What do you mean stolen? From the garage? We've used them for over thirty years – surely not? Your Dad swore by them. What did John say?'

'No! Someone else took my keys from their office.'

'Are you OK? Do you need me to come to pick you up?'

'No, you can't be seen with me. I don't want you dragged into all this.'

'Ian, dragged into all what?'

'Someone wants me dead because I'm uncovering the truth.'

Ian was not always like this – only in phases. He was generally independent, and he could look after himself. In fact, he took very good care of himself – eating a very specific diet, weighing foods, counting macronutrients, ordering organic products from specialised websites online. He often gave June food packages, referencing new information some friend of his had uncovered about what was really in supermarket food. Ian knew all sorts of information.

The internet had changed his life as a young teenager; forums, chat rooms, blogs, networks. He had begged them for broadband internet. Back then, even Edward (also an avid researcher, but with an office full of books), had been concerned of letting the internet invade their lives and homes.

Ian then went on to study Astrophysics at Durham University and wrote many of his assignments on extra-terrestrial phenomena. During that time, he had his accident: he fell from a first story balcony at a party, breaking his pelvis. He had relied on heavy pain medication, even now, eleven years later. Having spent all that time stuck inside in recovery, and desperate to finish his university course, Ian started an innovative project – a blog documenting all sorts of mysterious and murky things; government secrets, conspiracy theories, exposing covert military operations.

'So, what are you going to do Ian? What about the car?' she asked desperately, trying to make sense of it all.

'I'll call the police and get a crime number. But just to be safe, I'll make sure I use an alias.'

Wednesday 9th March 2016, 12.27 pm

As Ian crossed the road, he noticed a ginger tabby cat watching him. He had never really trusted cats, they always looked so suspicious. He eyeballed it but then lost focus as the need to look for oncoming traffic overtook him.

Ian walked into the police station. It was a modern building reimagined a few years ago when the old building had been bulldozed to the ground and in its place grew this overwhelming box of a building with more windows and edges than required.

The reception area was quiet. A woman was rummaging through her handbag at one of the windows, reassuring the receptionist that she had some sort of identification document. Sat on the few chairs to the left of the desk was a man, probably in his mid-thirties, dressed in painting overalls, a pained expression on his face. Ian chose not to take a seat, but to stand and wait his turn.

'Can I help?' the lady called to him after a short while.

'I need a crime number.'

'Ok then sir, what is it you are reporting?' replied the middle-aged woman.

'I'm reporting the theft of my car.'

'Ok then sir, are you able to fill in this form and I will arrange for someone to call you with a crime reference number?'

Ian took the form and started to read the information.

'Do you need a pen, sir?'

'Yes please.'

Ian took the form, and the pen, and began to fill in capital letters in little boxes. T-O-M. He had to go over the M a few times as the pen had stopped working. He tried to continue but the ink would not flow on to the paper. Ian muttered something under his breath.

'Do you have another pen, please?' he called out to the receptionist and continued to try engraving the letters on the form.

She smiled and offered him another one. Ian thanked her and returned to his form filling. He continued with the new pen.

T-O-M space H-I-N-D-S.

Wednesday 9th March 2016, 1.03 pm

The sky had darkened. Ian started to walk faster as fat drops of rain hit the back of his head. His phone started to vibrate in his pocket. He took shelter in a nearby shop front. It was his mum calling, again.

'Hello.'

'Ian, where are you?'

'I'm near the police station.'

'What are you going to do now? Do you need me to come and collect you?'

'Soon. I wanted to pick up something. I'll get a message to you.'

Ian pulled the collar of his jacket closer around his ears for a little extra protection against the rain. He walked quickly down a few streets, intentionally taking a couple of precautionary diversions before eventually arriving at the public library. He stopped briefly, noticing another ginger tabby cat. He thought it must have been the same cat; its markings were too similar to be a different cat. Was it following him? He tried not to hang about and stare at it. Instead, he quickened his pace and pushed through the doors of the library.

Ian headed straight to the books in the crime and detective aisle. He needed something comforting, something familiar, something to help him relax. It had to be a Raymond Chandler novel, of course. They were his favourites. From the shelf, he picked up one of two copies of *Farewell, My Lovely* and held it with both hands: a nostalgic pleasure, the soothing cold touch of the laminate of a library book. He flicked through the pages, planning to read a random page. But the page was decided for him, not by chance but by a singular post-it note.

There was a yellow square with a pencil-written comment: *Pick up a sketch of the past.*

Ian tried to understand the significance of the page, he scanned, but nothing immediately sprung out. Was it a message or just a coincidence? But surely it must be a clue. Either someone was helping him or being a hindrance. It would be a pretty sick joke using his favourite novel.

Involuntarily he thought of that cat again – its glaring eyes, those honeycomb eyes seemed to look straight through him. *Pick up a sketch of the past.* What did that mean? Maybe he was overthinking it. But, perhaps, it meant just that exactly. That is what he would do, then. Chalksey Antiques had been on the high street for 45 years and had been owned by three generations of the Chalksey family. Ian had browsed the shop regularly, largely due to his curiosity for historic artefacts. Tomorrow, he would go with a plan.

Thursday 10th March 2016, 11.14 am

The bell tinkled as he entered through the shop door. Behind a large old-fashioned cash register, sat a very tall, white-haired man in a checked shirt and corduroy trousers, reading a little green book with gold gilt. Mr. Chalksey had a friendly face: charming and gentle.

'Good morning,' said Mr. Chalksey as he looked up from his book.

'Hello,' he replied, immediately starting to browse to indicate that he didn't need any help.

Ian walked past the larger furniture, through an archway into another room. There were bookcases, mirrors, frames, and paintings. He looked at the artwork displayed on the walls. He had always had an interest in history, but he was mostly unknowledgeable about art and artists. Nevertheless, he could tell the difference between a sketch and a painting. He gently searched through a collection of frames that were stacked and scattered against bookshelves and dressers. There were oil paintings and photographs. But, there was only one sketched drawing.

It was of a sleeping woman with a diaphanous sheet draped across her torso and slipping off her toes. This must be it, Ian thought. It was the only sketch in the only antique shop in town.

Ian walked back to the gentle giant and presented the sketch to him. Mr. Chalksey stood up from his stool and took the sketch; cutting off the small white parcel tag attached to the frame and typed the same number into the cash register.

'That will be £85 then, please. Cash or card?'

'Cash, please. Would it be possible to pay a deposit and pay the full amount later this afternoon?' asked Ian.

'Our policy is to take a 20% deposit and keep it for 48 hours if you leave your name and number.'

'Yes please, I've got £15 in cash. Will that cover it?'

'Sure. What's your name and number?'

'Tom Hinds but I'll have to leave my mother's number with you. You'll be able to contact me through her.'

Ian wrote down the number with the pen and paper offered to him. He would call his mother and ask if he could borrow the cash as a small loan. She might ask why and worry he was having one of his paranoid episodes, but he would just have to reassure her that he was certain on this one.

Thursday 10th March 2016, 2.43 pm

June had made a fresh pot of tea in her favourite polka dot teapot – a wedding anniversary present from Rebecca. She sat down at the kitchen table and looked out on her garden, her happy place. She had been tidying up the potting shed this afternoon; it was too cold and windy to do anything in the garden. Her phone vibrated on her farmhouse-themed vinyl tablecloth. It was an unknown number – but local. Normally she would have ignored it but she trusted the local area code.

Swipe to Answer.

'Hello.'

'Oh, hello there, is Tom Hinds available to talk?' the voice replied.

'Can I ask who is calling, please?'

'Of course, it's David Chalksey from Chalksey Antiques.'

'Oh. Hello. I'll get him to call you back. Can I take a message?'

'Sure, it's regarding his purchase of *The Sleeping Woman*. We've had another interested buyer and I need him to confirm his intent to purchase.'

'Thank you,' she said, ending the conversation and hanging up.

June Valentine was not surprised. She was always curious about the incidents that only Ian seemed to be able to galvanise, but she was certainly not surprised. Of course, it could have been a wrong number, but it was not likely. Ian had often used code names for all sorts of things; it was part of his protection in his field of work. Apparently.

'Ian!' she shouted up the stairs.

'Yeah?'

'A David Chalksey just phoned for you. Do you want to call him back?'

Ian appeared at the top of the stairs.

'What did he say?'

'Something about *The Sleeping Woman*, and another buyer and your sale or something.'

'Another buyer?'

This was only a confirmation, Ian thought. Someone was on his scent now; he was sure of it. Were they after him? Or were they after the same thing? But what was he after? The sketch, the post-it note, the book, the car. He still wanted his car back, that is where it had all started, but that was probably collateral damage now. He had bigger fish to fry.

Thursday 10th March 2016, 3.06 pm

It was now paramount that Ian watched his every step. He had gone for a walk so that he could think more clearly. It was beginning to work when he was suddenly stopped in his tracks. He had been pacing the pavements when a cat – the cat – stood in the middle of the path and interrupted him. It was that ginger tabby cat, the one with the honeycomb eyes! Its suspicious look unnerved Ian, he had always had a dislike for cats, but this was one was especially haunting and persistent. It was those alluring eyes! The cat seemed to be becoming a regular visitor to Ian these days. The irony wasn't lost on Ian. It was his Dad who had always been the one with infinity with animals, especially with cats – 'they always seem so wise' his Dad would often say – 'and if only we could live a day in their life what would we learn?'

Ian reflected tenderly on his late father. He had been so inspired by his father's works – he was an advisor for government policy on environmental issues. He was so passionate about his works. That's where Ian got it from of course, but his mother seemed to think it was more paranoia than a passion. Why couldn't she be proud of him like she was of his father?

'Ian!' a voice called out. He carried on walking, refusing to acknowledge anyone in public, not at a time like this. Not now.

'Ian!' a voice so familiar now it was repeated. It was his mother.

'Not now, Mum, not now. I'll be back soon. I promise. Go back home, don't let anyone see you.'

'No Ian do not 'not now' me, not this time. I've seen this before; it's another one of your phases. But I won't let you, not this time. One of your important phases, I'm sure, but I can't lose you for another six months while you bury yourself under government secrets and conspiracy nonsense.'

'It's not nonsense Mum, I've told you before, you'll see. Please.'

'Yes, I'm sure. There's good in what you're trying to do, I get that, but I want my Ian Valentine back. Not Tom Hinds or any other alias. I need my Ian. I lost your father and I can't sit back and watch you go too.'

Ian was silent; he had no response to that. No matter how urgent this issue was, which it was, he would be sure to reiterate that to his mother at some point. But not now, like she had said, not now. He had to be her son now. He would have to wait. He would have to follow the clues later – he could give it a day or two. Right now, he didn't know what he was chasing anyway. He needed an anchor, a constant. That was what was so sticky about this one – he needed to figure out what was connecting all these happenstances. For now, though, he had better reassure his mother.

'You're right Mum. What I think we both need is some tea,' Ian said, putting an arm around her.

He glanced back. The cat was still sat there, watching.

'Mum, have you ever seen that cat before?'

She stopped and turned back to see for herself. She studied the cat carefully.

'It's Tybalt. She belongs to the Mable's at Number 37.'

'Are you sure she is a she? Tybalt is Juliet's male cousin.'

'What?'

'In *Romeo and Juliet*. Tybalt is Juliet's cousin.'

'Oh, maybe it is a male cat, then. You can ask Mr. Mable all about it if you like, he's coming to tune the piano tomorrow morning.'

Friday 11th March 2016, 10.52 am

'Would you like another cup of coffee Lawrence?' June asked.

'Yes, please, although I've got something to show you actually,' Mr. Mable replied from the lounge.

June poured another two coffees from her cafetière, adding a splash of milk in both mugs. She carried them both through to the lounge, where Mr. Mable was knelt down, surrounded by his tuning tools and dusters. As she walked in, he stood up from his collection of things, clutching a yellow duster with both hands.

'You might want to sit down for this one,' he continued.

June complied and took a seat on her sofa and lowered the mugs of coffee to the table.

'I'm all ears,' she said, with a naïve smile.

'I'm surprised I hadn't noticed it before. I have tuned this piano a good, what, ten times or more. But, in the back of it, I found a sort of secret cavity and in there, I found these.'

Mr. Mable handed over his yellow duster, which he was clasping like a moneybag. June peeled back the cloth to reveal a hoard of gold coins. She was speechless.

'They look old. You should take them somewhere to be valued,' Mr. Mable said.

'Who do they belong to?'

The piano was donated to Edward for his 60th birthday for his contribution to music in the community. Edward was a volunteer for a community band for over thirty years. He played the cornet.

'It's a beautiful Broadwood upright – even the piano is over 100 years old and would be worth over fifteen thousand pounds, and that's without considering the antique coins hiding in the back! You have some treasure in your hands here.'

Having overheard the conversation, Ian walked through the hallway and into the kitchen.

'What's this?' he asked.

Mr. Mable stayed quiet and let June explain.

'It's these coins. Lawrence just found them in the back of your father's piano. They could be worth something.'

'Let's have a look,' Ian said, offering his palms to receive them.

'These are old. They're gold sovereigns.'

'How old are they?' asked his mother.

'Hard to say. They're like the early £1 coins and they're still legal tender in Britain. They'll be worth a lot now, perhaps thousands if they're rare. Will you let me ask someone online?'

'Of course,' his mother replied.

Monday 14th March 2016, 2.45 pm

Ian had managed to value the coins pretty quickly; they were individually worth a few hundred pounds but collectively, easily more than a thousand pounds. Disturbingly, however, what had not gone away was the cat with those haunting honeycomb eyes. Ian knew how ridiculous it seemed, but ever since he had found the coins, he swore that the cat seemed to rarely leave the outside of their house now. His mother had noticed, but she assumed it must be the variety of sunny spots in her back garden. She liked cats, so long as they didn't destroy her garden, so she seemed uninterested in Ian's concerns when he asked her.

At first, he knew the rational explanation was that Mr. Mable's cat was fond of the back garden, just like his mother thought.

But after a few days, he noticed that he saw it night and day, sitting as though waiting for him.

Eventually, he waited for an opportune time when his mother was out of the house. Ian put his pride aside and decided to go and see the cat. He had reasoned that most cats would get spooked and run away, but not this one.

As he approached, the cat was watching him, as though it had been expecting him. It was languidly licking its front paw, slowly and carefully, obviously not a job to be rushed until satisfied. It slowly raised the now scrupulously clean paw in some sort of feline salute. When finally ready, the cat stared in his direction and concentrated his gaze upon Ian one last time as it readied to take its leave. The honeycombed eyes blazed brightly. It was as if an unspoken message was being transmitted between them. The only problem was Ian did not know what exactly the message was.

'Is this some sort of message?' he asked the cat, looking around to check no one was watching him talking so prescriptively to a neighbour's cat.

The cat's honeycomb eyes blinked and stepped towards Ian, wrapping his tail comfortably around Ian's legs. Ian stood and watched and waited. The cat, in one smooth movement, unravelled its tail from Ian's legs and walked into the house through the back door.

'Hey, Tybalt, stop!' Ian called.

The cat stopped and turned its head back to Ian. Could it understand him?

'If you can understand me, show me what I need to know.'

Ian thought he had gone too far this time. He hoped and prayed his mother would not come back from the shops any time soon. It would be enough to confirm another of his episodes.

The cat continued into the house and seemed to know where it was going. It darted up to his father's old office. Ian's mother had rarely touched this room since his father had passed away, retaining it as some sort of shrine that she allowed no one to disturb. The cat waited at the closed door, waiting for Ian to open it. He followed the silent orders. The cat jumped on the desk, and upon the multiple bookcases. It delicately and instinctively placed its paws without knocking anything, it weaved its way until it reached a folder on top of one of the bookcases. The cat knocked the folder and Ian quickly reacted. What was going on? Ian looked at the folder. He didn't remember seeing it before.

He picked it up and looked through it. There was a post-it note, directed to him: *Ian, keep investigating - please! Love Dad*.

Then underneath were numerous documents on Environmental Policy and court proceedings and a folder with the title 'The Prague Connection' emboldened across the front.

Ian looked back at the cat and felt an intense feeling of emotion; the cat's eyes blazed again.

'Dad? Is that you?'

The cat simply blinked while it licked its paw.

'Your final case I assume?' Ian said as he glanced at the now departing cat. '

A week later...
Monday 21ˢᵗ March, 7.01 am

June had been worried sick. She had tried to call Ian numerous times since she had received the text message in the middle of the night. But despite her efforts, there was still nothing. She had tried to get back to sleep about 3 am convincing herself that Ian would be fine. After all, he was an intelligent man, a well-connected man, a man who could stand on his own two feet. But she had still wrestled with her darkest thoughts all through the night. Finally, at 7 am, she eventually phoned Rebecca, knowing she would be up early to walk her dogs.

'I'm sorry for calling so early, but it's Ian.'

That was all she needed to say. In less than an hour, Rebecca was stood in her mother's kitchen boiling the kettle.

June tried to piece the bits together for Rebecca: his car was stolen; he had tried to buy a painting; the discovery of the gold coins and the need to have them valued.

'He took the gold coins?' Rebecca exclaimed.

'He said he was going to get someone to look at them. He said it would take a while to find the right person to get the right information. I figured it would take some time.'

'Do you know where he is now?'

'Last week, he phoned – last Tuesday I think it was – he said he was travelling to Prague to meet a friend called Vik. And something about your father's last case notes.'

'The text could have just been Ian exaggerating. You know how he is for stories, for drama.'

'But it said Dad can rest in peace now. What does that mean? What can we do?'

'Mum, there's not much we can do. Let me go and look in his room. I'll see what I can find,' said Rebecca, reassuringly patting her mum's arm as she left the kitchen.

In truth, Rebecca had no idea where to start either. Her brother's room was dark; he was not one to open his curtains. He had bad sleeping patterns anyway, spending copious amounts of time online in another reality, talking to people in other time zones. He also still suffered from bad bouts of pain and the medication would make him dehydrated, grouchy and give him bad migraines. She had to pull back the curtains to get some light in there.

Rummaging around Ian's desk, there was nothing obvious as some sort of clue. What was she even looking for? She opened a few drawers, looked in a few books, looked under the bed. But at the bedside table, she did find something. She picked up the yellow duster and looked at the gold coins for herself.

'Mum! The coins are still here.'

A week earlier...
Tuesday 15th March 2016, 12.55pm

Another day, another phone call. June picked up the iPhone vibrating and displaying Ian's name and picture. She was sat at the kitchen table with her eldest son, Michael.

'Hello,' she answered.

'Mum, this is going to be out of the blue and I can only apologise but I found Dad's last case notes. I have to go somewhere to get these documents in the right hands.'

'But Ian, where is somewhere?'

'To Prague, with a friend called Vik. I met her online but she's a good friend, honestly. She lives over there and she is going to put me up for a few days.'

'When will you be back?'

'As soon as I've finished what Dad started. I'm in a taxi on the way to the airport now. I have to go, Mum, but I'll be in touch!'

Before she could say anything, the line cut off.

'Why does he do this to you?' asked Michael.

'It's not his fault. He gets it from your father. He always had an interest in the mystical and the unexplained too,' his mother replied.

***

Edward Valentine had waited five long years to complete it; an important piece of investigative work that would finally expose another element of a secret and corrupt international collusion that he had been working on when he was cruelly snatched away from them. He licked his paw, turned around and went on his way. He now knew his son would be able to finish the job and get his message into the right hands. Not every coincidence had been a message for Ian, but either way, he could finish the work and Edward Valentine could now rest in peace.

A LONDON TRANSPORT ENCOUNTER

It's the day before Christmas Eve and I'm getting the train home for Christmas. I've not been home since the end of the summer, but a phone call and a letter have summoned me home. A lawyer's letter on the doormat at my flat informed me; something 'very important' and something about an inheritance. That part certainly piqued my curiosity.

I'm a financially impoverished Fine Art student: fur coat, Doc Martins, nose piercing. Am I that obvious? Probably. I look like I've swallowed the textbook and vomited all over myself. I'm a sticky stereotype.

I'm going home, near Birmingham, to see my family, as directed. I'm at London Euston. The train is very busy. Of course it is. It's on the 23rd of December. The day before Christmas Eve. The busiest day to travel, apparently. The very worst day to travel. Everyone is going home for Christmas or going somewhere to see someone; loved ones, hopefully. No one wants to be alone on Christmas.

Lots of people surge forward impatient to get on the train so I wait back a little. I can't be bothered to join the rabble. Pick your battles, Evelyn. I'm only travelling light, anyway.

I'll miss London within a few days, so I'll probably get a train back home on the 27th or the 28th at the latest, back for some 'killer' New Year house party. I swallow a bit of vomit in the back of my throat. I've packed a few clothes;

my makeup, a magazine and some hair straighteners. It's not exactly neatly packed; half of it is sort of spilling out, but it's zipped up to some degree. It's keeping up with the appearances, I suppose.

I eventually get on the train. At first, I casually wait in the doorway because a few people are standing by their suitcases. One guy is stood with a bike. Great: pedals in my calves, I think. But no, I've jumped to conclusions. There are still a couple of seats free. Hallelujah, that's a Christmas miracle. Luckily, no one else seems to move towards them. I sort of give people the eye without them noticing. No one is moving. Their humongous suitcases stand by them like giant memorial stones; cold, anchoring them to the spot. I make my way down the aisle. The train has started to move now so I do that balance-walk-steady thing to avoid tripping down the aisle or hitting someone with my bag. Subconsciously, I calculate my bodyweight against the speed of the train, steady but bottom-heavy in my oversized Doc boots. Without too much more drama, I make it to the first available seat and quickly sit down. I'm sat next to this old, lovely lady. I've sat down so quickly and smiled so charmingly – as is strongly advisable for old dears. I notice my cheeks hurt. I don't normally charmingly, Britishly, smile for old dears, or anyone. Not in London. It's nostalgic muscle memory for my face. All this happens in a split second: thinking, smiling, sitting, smiling, thinking. I've sat next to an old dear, yes. But I've failed to notice (in that split second of getting arse-to-seat as quickly as possible) that she is wearing the same coat as me. Great!

It's too late to move. And I've smiled at her. We're practically stitched together now. It's a peculiar London transport encounter. As I rationalise all of this, my eyeballs fix on the seat in front of me. People can see us. The ghost of Christmas Past and Present sat together on the 12:23 train to Birmingham New Street.

Great!

OK. We're just wearing the same coat. So perhaps it's not a big deal. It's fine for her. I mean, she's probably loving it, if she's even noticed. Probably not. She's doing a crossword. It's fine. It's in fashion. It's a total overreaction. I feel stupid. I start to settle and soften my gaze. I relax and suddenly feel a fondness for her. We've already shared a smile after all, and now we can share the same coat. What the hell? We look good. I try and study her as subtly as possible. I notice that she has a cute bag. Vintage is a lie. I want it. Her left hand is clutched through the handles of the bag. Like she's protecting it from a mugging. Keeping her bag safe. That pang of fondness returns, over-powering this time.

Her hands are old and frail – like my grandmother's hands were. My grandmother was a very successful painter. I'm following in her artistic footsteps, although she probably wouldn't approve of my sculptures, or maybe she would love them! I'm not so sure. The memories of my Grandma, all of them, come flooding in, and my eyes well up. I want to know more about my travelling companion, to know her story. And so now, ridiculously, I'm sat on a crowded train, the day before Christmas eve, trying to not lose my mind and now I'm crying about an old dear sat next to me, who is wearing my coat, who I envy and love in equal measure and care for and want, to nurture, to love, to understand. This is just weird.

I just sit for some time. Painfully enjoying all the memories of my grandma and pretending this old lady could have been her. Or, that I could have been this woman's granddaughter.

She keeps her hands tightly clutched through her handbag at all times, other than when she gets something out; cheese and onion crisps, her train ticket, a sandwich, a crossword book, a word search book, her pen. I hope she's returning home to a family that loves her. A family that tells her they love her, frequently and often; that appreciates every bone in her body, every hair on her head, every intricacy, every anxiety, every irrational habit. I hope she's going somewhere for Christmas. But, why does she travel from London Euston, alone, on the busiest day of the year?

This unexpected vulnerability moved me to say something.

'Hello,' I said to her.

'Oh, hello. I was a little distracted there,' she said putting down her pen.

'Are you going to Birmingham for Christmas?' I replied.

'Oh, I'm going to a little place outside Birmingham. A little village, I've got it written down somewhere. Gilson. I'll need to order a taxi when I get to the train station.'

She's going to the same place as me!

'That's a coincidence. I know the village, very well.'

'I have a lawyer's letter in my handbag telling me about my twin sister. A sister I don't remember that well as I spent my childhood in care, but it seems she never forgot about me! According to the letter, she's left me a sizeable share of her estate.'

Were our reasons for travelling on a busy noisy train connected?

'Do you know the family? The Simpsons?' she asked.

'Know them? That's my grandmother's name!'

'Hilda Simpson?'

'Yes!'

'That's my sister's name, Hilda. I'm Doris. We were put in care when we were just days old. She found adoptive parents, but I wasn't so lucky. I never did know what happened to her – until now. Look at this letter. It tells me I've inherited a part share of her estate.'

I studied the letter. It was from the same firm of lawyers and it contained the same details as the letter I had received. Did this mean this dear old lady was going to have a share of my grandmother's estate?

As the journey to Birmingham progressed, we continued to talk and learn more about each other and our bizarre connection.

***

It was late by the time when we both boarded the last local train; two travellers wearing the same coat; one without a penny to her name and one with a vintage handbag to die for. Thankfully this train was much quieter.

We both stepped down onto the deserted platform. It was late now and although the mainline had been busy, not many travelled this rural route on Christmas Eve's eve. We climbed over the bridge to reach the exit gate on the other side of the station. It was already dark. Doris shuffled slowly along the edge of the platform.

'What a surprise this whole journey has been!' Doris said.

'Yeah – hasn't it just!' I replied.

The late-night freight train approached heading in the other direction. From experience, I knew that it thundered through the station barely slowing, as this was only a small village station. My mind raced. Thoughts flooded through my mind at a speed almost as fast as the approaching train. I quickly realised it was now or never. Any inaction would condemn me to a lifetime of being a struggling Art Student. Should I? Could I?

With an imperceptible, almost reckless action, I grabbed hold of Doris.

'Watch out, auntie Doris. This train comes steaming through!'

'Oh goodness! Thank you,' she said, wrapping her hands around her frail body and patting my cold hands. It was like my grandmother's touch; well, of course, she was about the closest thing to my own grandmother!

'You won't believe this,' I said, 'but I bet you haven't even noticed that we're wearing the same coat?'

She stopped and took her own assessment of our garments.

'Well, I never. Do you believe in Fate, Evelyn?'

'Today, I do.'

SCULPTURES

Sculptures haunted Hugo. Their fractured torsos; the fleshy marble; many disproportionate figures; the gigantic commodity; the minute embodiment; their mirrored forms cold to touch. Hugo now spent many of his working days, almost every part of them, stood or sat next to a sculpture.

A brook trickled behind the pale walls of the gallery and it often reminded Hugo of his childhood, where he would play pooh sticks over a precarious bridge near their little house. How much can change in the course of a man's life? He would think this to himself as he stared into the water; he listened to its relentless movement over rocks and debris and thought deeply about how this gallery, this one space on earth, had completely saved his life.

Hugh Sterling was better known as Hugo and for reasons never officially revealed to him. It was probably something to do with his olive skin, dark black hair and hairy arms; he looked Mediterranean but as far as he was aware, he was Scottish. He preferred the name Hugo anyway.

'It's far more metropolitan don't you think?' he once asked Saskia.

They'd become friends throughout many coffees; every one of them purchased by Hugo as part of his daily, and now, long-established, routine. Every morning on his way to work at the City Art Gallery, he called into Saskia's coffee shop. It was decorated with a variety of colourful chairs (some were metal, and others wooden); Indian textiles and homemade art, mostly postcard-sized watercolour paintings, coloured the walls. Hugo thought they were truly beautiful. He thought the whole shop was beautiful, including Saskia.

'If you say so Hugo. I like it if you like it,' Saskia replied.

A sharp breeze in the morning, strong dark coffee and the bright colours of Saskia's shop brought an essential serenity to Hugo's working day. It marked every weekday morning and structured his working week. Saskia was probably his best friend.

Anthony, his longest-serving friend and the best man at his wedding, was probably supposed to be his best friend, by the rules, but in truth, he had very little in common with Anthony besides drinking a beer or two on a summer afternoon. Hugo liked Anthony and he liked Hugo. They were still very good friends and had helped each other out significantly, but Hugo found Saskia was much easier to talk to. Besides, Anthony was ever more preoccupied with his teenage daughters and an ever more demanding Labradoodle named Buddy these days.

For almost eight years, Hugo had worked at the gallery. He'd started as a cleaner – although those first few months now seemed like they belonged to a previous life of Hugo's. He took the job on his fortieth birthday – a small victory that he had managed to battle alone; a small victory that was a long time since his first and only job before the gallery. Back then, he had received a phone call on his sixteenth birthday from Mr. White.

'There's a job at the factory if you want one. You can start on Monday at 8 am. Don't be late.'

Hugo spent the next twenty-two years working his heart out at a food factory in his hometown. It was a pleasant enough life. He got married at twenty-four, to a pretty girl named Yvonne, the youngest daughter of the pub's landlord, a family friend. Hugo was a quiet soul, working hard six days a week and playing cards and drinking beer with Anthony on a Sunday afternoon. Yvonne had many more friends than Hugo. She was kind-hearted enough; she earned friends running errands all day, but she was obsessed with town gossip and as it turned out, she had a few too many close friends; very close friends!

Hugo was never sure he handled the situation correctly. He had never really understood women. He did not even see his mother as a woman, but always and forever, only, as his mother. He had tried to raise his voice to Yvonne when her affair(s) became public knowledge.

'You think you can just walk all over me, Yvonne.' It was more of a stern comment than a challenge. 'Well, you can't. I'm your husband. Does that mean anything to you?'

They were all the words that he could muster to challenge her. He was deeply upset and there was a dark pit in his stomach. He'd never had mastery over his own words. They never made an appearance when he felt he needed them most. Sadly, despite his valiant effort, Yvonne looked neither phased nor bothered. There were a few moments of icy silence before she answered him coldly and said, 'it doesn't mean anything, not anymore.' It was as though she'd rehearsed her line already. Without further hesitation, she turned dramatically on her heels and left through the front door. Hugo never saw her again.

Following that, Anthony had persuaded Hugo, at age thirty-eight, to move to the city to begin living a new life. And he did. He moved into Anthony's flat and initially, spent most of it lying depressed in bed. Meanwhile, everything about Anthony's life was getting better by the day. He'd found a job as a waiter in some posh hotel and was well on his way to promotion within months of being there.

'People move around all the time in hospitality. I'll be a manager in no time.'

He was right. He was happier than ever and was soon promoted to Hospitality Manager at The Royal Hotel. He fell in love with one of the receptionists and they bought a house together in the leafy suburbs of the city. Leaving Hugo, alone, and living in Anthony's flat.

***

There was nothing he could compare to the feeling of being alone on one of the gallery floors. Each floor was a world of its own, four or five rooms, wide-open spaces with big arches linking through from one to the other. He got lost a few times in his first weeks, scared of pulling the vacuum cleaner six feet behind him and knocking over something important. He liked to look, but he'd never touch, he'd never dare. He was one of three cleaners and there were five floors. The other two were older ladies and he thought it kind that he should clean the top two floors. Secretly, it was because he longed to be with all the statues on the top floor. He later learned the correct term was not a statue, but a sculpture.

The room was littered, intentionally, with materials of all kinds – some barely recognisable as any sort of familiar shape – but mostly with dark human forms. They were sometimes vulgar and yet the most extraordinary things Hugo had ever experienced.

On his walk home, his mind would tick over and over, searching for the right expression to describe this feeling he felt while immersed in the gallery.

'I can't explain it to you, Anthony. It's like a room full of not-ghosts, not-people, but feelings and forms, or something.' He had never been good with words.

'It sounds a bit deep to me, mate,' said Antony.

They were a simple sort of people; they were used to saying it how it was. Or saying nothing at all. Hugo would have difficulty explaining how to cook his dinner, let alone about how he felt about modern art. He'd never thought about art before, especially not how it made him think or feel.

Sometimes the gallery put on special late-night sessions with artists and academics. Hugo would have to stay later to clean and he rarely had a clue what they were talking about. He knew exactly how Anthony felt. He too thought most of it was nonsense, deep – and, even a bit pretentious. He had hoped they might have offered him more insight at one of these evenings; insight into how he could explain it – the presence those sculptures had; the way each one of them was full of an emotion that he could very almost, but never quite, put next to a memory of his. One reminded him of how he felt when Yvonne walked out. Another reminded him a bit like how he felt when his mother died. One was a bit like how he felt when he first moved to the city and couldn't make sense of any of it. The only person he felt he could explain these thoughts to was Saskia.

'But that's the sublime nature of art Hugo, it's uniquely both beautiful and powerful, it reveals every shade of humanity – dark and light,' she said.

Hugo didn't answer her. He was silent, deliberating on what she'd said but, in that time, Saskia had moved on to take the order of a young couple at the table over by the window.

Eight years on from his job cleaning the gallery, Hugo was now a security guard there. The gallery had a lot of its funding cut, losing staff and all to the War outside its precious walls and artefacts. On his first day as a security guard, he'd specifically requested if he could patrol around floor five.

'Why is that Hugo?' Felix asked.

His manager was a nice posh man, in his late twenties, called Felix. He wore a waistcoat, colourful stripy socks, a bow tie, and thick-rimmed glasses.

'It's the sculptures. I really like them, but I can't quite describe why,' Hugo replied. Felix smiled a big smile and nodded his head.

'I didn't know you were so into art Hugo.'

Hugo didn't know whether that was a question or not.

'I don't know anything about art but those sculptures, they're not like anything I've felt before.'

Felix chuckled but didn't say anything. Perplexed, Hugo thought perhaps he should not have requested a specific floor in the first place, perhaps that was too bold a request, especially so soon after a great promotion.

'Floor five is all yours Hugo,' replied Felix.

Hugo was thrilled. He could now spend all day roaming to and fro, room to room. He worked as hard as ever. He was mindful of everything happening in the gallery, though there was rarely any trouble in a place like that. People generally spoke in whispers. They mostly just stopped to look, admire and appreciate. Sometimes he'd purposely mirror the thoughtful looks of others: mostly just for fun, but he was also intrigued as to how others looked at the sculptures. Was there a right way to look at the form, the shape, the expression? Hugo had decided the answer was no. Every day he looked at them a bit differently, but he never felt wholly the same way about them.

'Do you have a favourite?' Saskia had asked him one day on his way back from work. Every so often he'd pass by to pick up some milk from Saskia.

'They change the sculptures every few months or so, with each new exhibition season. I miss some and others I've probably forgotten about. I don't know about favourites. I've never thought about them that way you know.'

The next day Hugo made a deliberate point of spending time by a different sculpture. He spent fifteen minutes by each one studying and scrutinising before strolling on to the next one. He made sure not to do it in any specific order to keep moving around all the rooms as freely and widely as possible, so still keeping to his allocated areas of responsibility. There was rarely any trouble anyway. He'd made sure there were no school trips booked in today, so the likelihood of any disturbance was minimal. At the end of the day, he'd try and decide which one was his favourite in this particular exhibition. However, it was no easy decision. Each one was so different. No matter how much they haunted, confused and disturbed, they also enlightened and inspired. He finally forced himself to shortlist three in his mind. He was never any good at remembering names of artists or sculptures, so he nicknamed them in his head: *Bag of Bones, Mr. Hunch*, and *Woman in Pain*.

The first was made of brown rusty material and the body was only represented structurally, like rusty bones. Hugo thought it weird because although it conjured up ideas of rusty old car parts, it also looked like it was drooping, hanging, like it was a heavy piece of flesh. He didn't know how the artist had done it; it was like a rusty old bag of bone and muscle.

Mr. Hunch, on the other hand, was a very tall scary-looking clay man. He was a dark green, hazy-grey colour. There were fingerprint marks in his cheeks, shoulders, and knees. Hugo wasn't sure what it was supposed to mean but he felt strongly that it meant something. The sculpture was powerful and hunched over and Hugo couldn't tell if he should feel scared of him or sorry for him.

His last choice was the one he named *Woman in Pain*; a feminine figure was broken in material, position, and expression. He felt himself wanting to comfort the woman, to put his hand on her shoulder or something. He felt stupid when he remembered it was just a cold piece of stone. All three sculptures had especially made him feel something and he liked the power they had evoked from somewhere deep inside. The artist must be proud of that, he thought.

'You don't have to choose a favourite Hugo,' Saskia said, later, when he confessed that he still couldn't choose.

'But I want to choose one,' he lamented.

Hugo sat engrossed in deep brooding thought as he let his coffee go cold. Saskia went to make him a replacement one.

'I think it should be the *Bag of Bones* one,' he eventually shouted across to her. She quickly popped her head out from behind the coffee machine.

'And why is that?' she asked.

'I can see myself in it. There's a difference between what people see in me and what I see about myself. The sculpture is just a rusty bag of bone and muscle, and that's what it looks like, but it's so much more than that isn't it?'

'Yes, Hugo,' she replied, 'it's what you see that counts. No one else can see what you see. That's what makes art so personal.'

FIN DEL MUNDO (THE END OF THE WORLD)

El Principo

'What can you do about the rattlesnakes?' I asked innocently, as we both stood outside, looking at the ramshackle building.

I could see that both my question and I appeared to have an unpleasant effect on him. The balding estate agent pulled at his collar in a poor attempt to relieve some of his awkwardness.

'Well, you could keep the vegetation in the yard to a minimum, and the trash in check,' he sheepishly replied.

I looked at him disapprovingly. I never had a way with people and this social situation was not likely to be any different. People exhausted me. Twenty years in New York were enough to kill me: three times over. That was the whole point of moving here, wasn't it? A solitary retreat. An eternal escape from the tiresome world. I get on really well with myself, most of the time.

'I'll buy it,' I declared. I probably earned that man a promotion for selling that desolate place and good for him, although he deserved nothing of it. Such is life.

I stood, motionless in the garden, gazing at one of my unkempt flowerbeds. Mesmerized as they moved – nodding, despite any wind. I am sure that as I stared, they began to pulse, to almost dance. I took an opportunity to just watch the flowers dance in the wind. The pale colors became vivid, a fountain of color trickled. Rigorous patterns melted into waves of oil paint. At that moment I became fixated; it became my whole world. I have never really been interested in flowers, but I often paint them. Besides, they're far easier to paint than models are in my experience.

New Mexico was the new place to call my home. The Land of Enchantment. I had already decided to call my ranch 'Fin Del Mundo'; the end of the world. This was my pursuit of happiness; both the end of myself and the start of a new part of me. I loved New Mexico. It gets about 310 glorious days of sunshine a year; vast, infinite landscapes and more importantly; low humidity. Not enough people appreciate what a beautiful thing low humidity is. It means my hair is flat and manageable rather than wild and frizzy; mould doesn't grow; dust mites can't survive; cheaper utility bills; the bathroom mirror doesn't fog up and instead I can see myself as I really am – a crisp, clear and pale reflection. And most of all, the paint dries really quickly. Have I told you I moved here to paint already? I'm a painter. It's what I do. It's who I am.

I am terrified of small spaces after an age in New York, but this little house was very different. It was my own space, an enchanted ranch house with so much light. It had this great, white feeling about it – a blank canvas if you like. Inside, it was shabby and cold but the way the light came in through the crooked windowpanes made the whole place come alive. It's a gloriously humble place to live and work: to paint and to sleep. I could imagine growing raspberries in the garden before I'd even signed the contract. So I guess, yes, as the estate agent had said, I would have to keep the vegetation to a minimum and 'in check' as he'd so politely put it. He didn't know how appropriate his comment had been. I'd have to keep a lot of things in check. Myself included.

'I haven't any glasses. I don't use them,' I told the estate agent as he led me inside, sitting down at the worn, wooden kitchen table. There was limited furniture inside. The kitchen table was in awful condition; bleached of all its original color.

'Do you have any glasses you could use for the purpose of reading and signing the documentation, Madam?' he looked at me, embarrassed. I hated that he called me Madam. I hate formalities altogether.

'No. But what fool can't sign their name on a dotted line?' I smirked at him as he began to wipe his sweaty forehead on the back of his bony hand.

I couldn't bear the thought of unpacking and so I never really did. I picked essential pieces of furniture that I had asked my good friend Frank to drive to the ranch in his truck. I heaved in a few cases and a small collection of boxes and things (mostly photographs, books, and my canvas-making materials). It was just important things to me really – things I enjoyed or things I couldn't bring myself to part with. My life in New York was full of insignificant things that I did not want to bring with me – ridiculous cushions, fancy lampshades and scented candles that made me feel nauseous and trapped inside some lifestyle magazine. Give me vast empty spaces I tell you! So, I had very little to unpack when I arrived. My books reordered themselves in convenient piles across the ranch house depending on what I fancied reading on that day, at that time, in which light. Moving to New Mexico was the new life I'd been eager to kickstart, and I had started almost immediately on a project I'd been desperate to work on for years but it was never feasible with limited space in New York.

I had been interested in classic cars for a long time; it had been something my uncle had introduced me to when I was about seven years old and I spent many summers sitting around, talking, watching what he was doing with different tools and car parts. I was a young and placid child with a very little yearning for anything, or at least that's what my mom told me. I can imagine I was just intensely bored and secretly there was a deep passion to escape and experience my own adventures that were burning inside my young, little, feeble body.

My inspired project was a 1929 Model AA: a heavy-duty truck variant of the Ford Model A. It was a revolutionary vehicle in its time – selling millions and a huge success for Ford. I bought it from a recommended dealer in Jacksonville. He was an expert in his field and clearly knowledgeable when I spoke to him on the phone before I went to see it for myself. He had been trading classic cars for over forty years and I had a gut feeling that my uncle would have trusted him with his life, although, I don't think I could trust any sort of salesmen. But then I am a professional pessimist.

'What does a good lady like yourself want with a classic motor like this?' he'd commented as I handed over the money – cash is king, obviously. He only had the cheek to ask me once my money was firmly in his hand, judging critter! I was interested to see whether the old boy could count money and listen at the same time. I told him my restoration plans, my escape to New Mexico, the dream my uncle had instilled in me from a young age. To drive wild, open landscapes in a restored vehicle was the closest thing to freedom I could think of after my suffocating life of Fine Art in New York. He looked at me blankly, as though I had somehow absent-mindedly handed him paper money. Although come to think of it, I probably should have just told the man what he half-expected to hear...

'It's not for me. I'm just running an errand for my sweet, old Papa.'

What the hell did it matter that I, a woman, wanted a classic motor? What makes a car a man's object and a stove a woman's object? Living in a man's world is not the real problem, its being in a man's world and having everything you do viewed through the conventions of one outdated 'perfect' idea of a woman; why could a man be whatever he wanted to be? I could live quite happily in a man's world if I weren't constantly being reminded that I was merely a woman within it. It tires me out, just like the art world, and New York had finally destroyed me. I could no longer face art dealers: art as a commodity, art as exchange. How about Art for Art's sake? Woman for Woman's sake?

I bought the truck anyway and had it towed back to my yard. I worked on it tirelessly. Most days followed a similar routine: wake up naturally, as the sunlight beamed across my bedroom; throw some clothes on (jeans, an oversized shirt, sandals); take a walk around outside (there was plenty of space of course); walk up an appetite and cook something for breakfast (eggs, bagels, fruit); paint most of the morning (the sunshine would move to the other side of the house by the afternoon). Then I would swap my paintbrush for a spanner. The garage was cool at the back of the house and I could forget about everything when I was in there. I'd work on my beloved Ford for about four hours on most days. When I reached a tight spot and I was unsure of my own ability, I'd call Frank and he would guide me through the next stage. Frank was a decent, kind of man like that.

I met Frank at a house party in New York. I detested parties, as you can probably imagine, but you might say it was an occupational hazard: 'Gee, you're an artist; to sell your work you must also sell yourself. It's New York, networking is partying!'

Frank was the husband of a wealthy art collector – it was all in her stockbroker family (old-money, though). Felicity Bloomberg met Frank Asher (the son of a lawyer and a doctor) on holiday in the Sunshine State. They were young and flirty, what else do people expect of you in your twenties when you're rich, good-looking and carefree? Frank and Felicity fell in love quickly – probably somewhere between the copious amounts of red wine and their mutual desperation to go to New York University. Frank wanted to study Politics or Economics and Felicity wanted to study Literature. They moved but Felicity never enrolled. Instead, she worked as a personal assistant to a senior broker at an investment bank, Mr. Stein. Frank chose to study Politics but struggled to find his opinion amongst all the white noise of other wealthy, naive undergraduates. After graduating, he took a job in a business consultancy firm and he hated it. They married two years later, and Felicity made sure they knew all the right sorts of people. She would arrange their diary with precision and fervor: dinner parties, cocktail evenings and charity fundraiser balls. Frank is a sociable man with the sharpest sense of humor, so for him, it probably wasn't all that bad, if only to meet such a fascinating, eclectic group of people. There was always someone he had never met before – a baseball player, a poet, an astronaut – the novelty did not wear off for years. He was a simple man but he appreciated the art of conversation and the arrangements that Felicity planned allowed him to live in a world of interesting people. It was at one of those parties that he encountered me. And that's how Frank Asher and I met. But, to cut a long story short, Felicity and Frank divorced after sixteen years of marriage.

It was another one of their mutual decisions – she wanted luxury and he wanted laid back and make-do. They both recognized it was an incompatible combination. They still meet up each year back in New York, but Frank wanted out of the big city as I did. We found a mutual connection in how much we had hoped and dreamed about New York, only to feel undersold. Nevertheless, I loved his stories and would often listen to them as he helped me fix the Ford.

It was all coming together: the painting, the truck, and all that space I needed. It took me about five months. I was adding the finishing touches and it was only some of the cosmetic touches left.

La Mitad

The sky was a perfect shade of blue: gorgeous and docile. It swallowed me up. Anxiety would often creep into my mind's space like an uninvited and unwelcome guest. Like any guest, you feel obliged to pay attention to them but really you cannot wait for them to leave so that you can get on and think clearly again. Or is that just me?

Anxiety has always been under my skin, creeping around. To be honest with you, I don't detest it at all. I think it has a very effective function. It's perfectly fine – helpful even – for analyzing all those worries and concerns we chase around our heads. The problem is when it not only thinks there's a problem but designs it in full color, high definition, with multiple dimensions so that the problem becomes an overpowering sculpture standing so tall that you can no longer work out what is real and what is imaginary.

'Were there any signals?' the psychiatric nurse asked me, coldly.

'I don't think there were any, but I never recall anything before a breakdown.'

They asked me to start wherever, so I started my story when I moved to the ranch in New Mexico.

New York induced regular mental breakdowns, so this was no amateur performance. I remember feeling those adrenalin surges rush through me. It felt very similar; the acid feeling of something sprinting to your fingertips, bypassing your organs and starving you of breath in your lungs. I felt clammy and I remember feeling tired and dreary, but I thought that was fairly normal.

'There were days, when I just longed to sleep, to sleep forever,' I replied to the psychiatric nurse, dolefully smiling at me.

I don't remember how it all happened, just that I suddenly needed to disconnect, to leave. I couldn't tell you that at the time but that black cloud I thought I'd left in New York seemed to have followed me. It found me when I thought I'd cut all ties with it. But it was my own shadow after all.

I had been in the garage, checking the brakes and I started to become overwhelmed by this need to sleep. The engine was still running and then I disconnected altogether. That's where Frank eventually found me and called 911.

Sadly, I have seen very little of that beautiful blue sky I loved so much. It's been 57 days now. I miss my ranch, my new sanctuary, god-forbid my actual Fin Del Mundo!

I had nearly finished the Ford, ready to drive the beauty, but here I am, cooped up, again. I've counted every day with boredom and bitterness. If I had it within me, I would have abandoned the cold bedsheets and run away, back to the ranch and driven away into the wild. I wouldn't even take my paints. To hell with it, I am done. I have often thought about running, but of course, I have not done it. I plague my mind with thoughts of it, but my body always thinks it's a lot of work, too much effort. It's such a nuisance; the way we long for these things and yet also feel paralyzed to do anything vaguely pro-active.

My therapy here is holistic, as they call it. It includes exercise, meditation, cleaning, (painful) group sessions, and what they call creative therapy: art, poetry, drama, photography, journaling, and sometimes they even wheel in a projector and show an 'appropriate' film for those in the session. I don't know who gets to censor that decision, but I do wish they would pick some more exciting films. I suggested *One Flew Over the Cuckoo's Nest* but apparently, that was 'by definition, inappropriate'. At least I still have my sense of humor I reassured the concerned nurse.

The journaling sessions were dull at first, but after some resistance, I was strongly advised to try it out, and somehow I got a bit lost in all the writing. The notebooks were small and bound by black leather (no expense spared!) and I was so attracted to their blank pages that I first started to draw abusive doodles across them, and then slowly, I started to write words with meaning. It was about working with the blankness of the page, not avoiding it or losing it, but whispering words onto blank pages. This is what power a writer must feel. Now they have asked me if I would like to continue to record my story, a way of processing the steps, a beginning, middle, and an end. I guess I'd call this part the middle and just so you know, I'm planning an excellent ending for you all. It will be the day I get that Ford back on the open road.

They have allowed me to paint as part of my therapeutic process, of course, but their paints are awful and watery.

'What do you love about painting?' the art therapist asked me in the first session.

I repeatedly rolled the therapist's question around my head. Having the therapist ask me that felt strange and uncomfortable.

'Is it about what you see or what you do?' she remarked.

'It's the way a painter sees the world,' I say, unsure of why I answered her like that. She looked at me, waiting for me to continue.

'People always think painting is the finished product. But that's missing the point. It's the process – it's just as much about the canvas, the white space, and the color. It's mixing the paint, too. That's really important. You have to mix the paint. So many people are afraid to mix the paint.'

***

They discharged me on a Tuesday. Weirdly, I felt uncomfortable about that because it was not the beginning of a week – but I took it anyway. Beggars can't be choosers.

Frank had offered to collect me. I packed my few meagre possessions – the clothes I was wearing the day I was hospitalized (oily green overalls that I had asked them to keep safe), some loose change and my six little, precious leather black notebooks. One of which I write this in now.

'You need to take it easy Ms. O. You'll need to give yourself time to rebuild your confidence,' she cooed as she closed my open window. By the open window, I mean an annoyingly tiny vent, which was utterly pointless, but it was considered a safety hazard in case I decided to end it all and jump. Ha! What was I? A contortionist?

I thanked her all the same, but I was sickly desperate to return to the ranch – to my raspberry bushes, to my own paints, and to my beloved Ford.

Frank was early, thank God. He knew I'd be growing impatient by the minute and even bought me a takeaway coffee from a nearby café. He walked through reception, hugged me and whispered in my ear.

'I've got a little surprise for you outside.'

I smiled a big smile and grabbed my bags and eagerly led us through the door. I was astonished to find he'd arrived to pick me up in my Ford.

'I hope you don't mind. I thought it would cheer you up. I know you can't drive yet but at least it's all finished and ready for you.'

'Frank,' I said and stopped to admire the finished work. I was so happy inside, but I could not say much. Frank knew I wouldn't want to talk much so he understood when all I could say was: 'Thank you.'

Frank drove us home and we barely talked. He asked whether I needed anything picking up from the grocery store and I said I'd probably need some basics. At some point, I would need more painting materials too. He offered to bring them round later. For someone who enjoyed the art of conversation, I was always astounded that he accepted our long silences when I knew he wanted to ask so many questions. I wondered whether I should let him read these journals – not all of them, but offer him snippets, perhaps read them to him as part of my continued therapy. I was looking out of the window, feeling comfortably dwarfed by the horizons thrown up by the vast landscapes of New Mexico. But now, as I sit and reflect and write this now, I realize Frank does not need to see these journals. He understands my silence and that is the importance of some friendships. It's the blank space amongst the brush strokes that makes your life a work of art.

El Fin

A couple of months later, I was feeling strong and ready. I had been given the go-ahead to drive again if I felt confident enough. This was the happy ending I'd been planning for so long. Thinking about it now though, it was a bad day to ride the motor. I had wanted a break from painting as my wrists were starting to ache. I'd thrown all my energy into crafting my canvases and painting them again – and these were bigger canvases than I had ever painted before. After being cooped up inside, I had moved some of them outside and tried painting in the garden. It was pleasant watching the paint dry so quickly, but I became dehydrated very quickly.

I had no real need to drive anywhere so I decided I'd just go for a short ride. I would drive a few miles to the gas station, pick up a coffee and drive it back again. The Ford started with the engine sounding like the purr of a wild animal and it genuinely excited me to be back behind the wheel. All those long hard hours I had spent fixing it up started to come back to me. Was this really the first time I would get to drive her on an open road?

We were off and the first few miles to the gas station went so quickly that I did not feel like stopping for a coffee, so I carried on and very quickly, a few miles became ten miles to the highway. Although I knew that was a bad idea, I told myself clear instructions: *Gee, remember what you keep being told. Set yourself realistic goals. Don't run before you can walk.* And I actually listened to myself for once. I took a left at the junction and drove back towards the ranch.

Don't run before you can walk. I repeated it as a mantra through my mind. But I was driving, not running or walking, and I wanted to keep driving – so I drove past the ranch and headed for the vastness of the wide, open roads. The sense of freedom was addictive and it coursed through my veins. However, a number of miles later, the engine started to splutter and misfire a few times and I realized I'd soon be further away from anywhere than I had gasoline in the tank to get me back home. Confusingly, the gauge indicated I still had a quarter of a tank left but I thought I had better check the engine to be sure. I stopped and checked but I could see nothing obvious. I turned the truck around and headed back towards the ranch so that I could get home safely. I'd already had too much fun for one day.

My fun had barely begun though as before I was even halfway home, the truck stopped altogether. Not now! Not here! Damn! I was out of gasoline and I should have thought about all of this. *Don't run before you can walk, Gee.*

I tried the ignition again, but it was hopeless: it produced nothing more than an endless whirling noise. What was I to do? Find a phone and call Frank? Call emergency services? I did not know what to do. I could walk back to the last payphone, which I reckoned must have been at least three miles ago. Or, I could walk to the nearest ranch, but even that was about five miles away. What to do? I thought. This crisis should have been averted. I had not learned my lesson. In the absence of any other plan, I started to panic.

I got back in the truck. I recall starting to shake and my thoughts becoming dark and clouded.

No. Gee! Hold on. Hold on. You've got options. You've always got options.

It was no good. I started to close my eyes and drift to some other place. Then I heard a strange noise from beside me, as though something had fallen. My neck suddenly twisted before my eyes had time to process what it was. Initially on the passenger seat, but now slithering in the footwell, was a baby rattlesnake – its flat, triangular head stirring from its slumber; his head was circling as I stared right into his beady eyes. He must have sneaked a lift while the truck was parked up at my house. For now, the matter of how he got there was academic. What was I to do now? Luckily, he did not raise his tail or present himself as an immediate danger, but it would only be a matter of time before he or I felt threatened and rattled in fear.

I have since had time to process it and as I write this, I am struggling to recreate my emotional state for you. One moment I was ready to break down like I'd done many times before, and the next moment I was forced to react. My first option was to get out of the vehicle, lay down in the sunshine and drift away. But with a venomous foe around, that was unwise and a life-limiting option. By some miracle, I chose another option. That made me as mad as a cut snake, as they say.

Nothing ventured, nothing gained. Blank space, brush strokes. Breathe in, breathe out. I calmed myself down.

I slowly manoeuvred myself out of the driver's seat, opened the door beside me and walked around the Ford and opened the door nearest the rattlesnake. I climbed on to the hood of the truck, crouched on all fours and watched patiently through the windscreen, all the while avoiding eye contact with my predator. The hood began to burn my kneecaps so I began to alternate between crouching and kneeling, continuing to fixate on where the snake was and what it would do next whilst performing some strange dance on what had once been my prized project but had now, all too quickly, become another death-trap.

After a while, the snake eventually opted for the warmer option and scuttled out of the truck and scurried across the sandy road, as quick as it could before finding a rocky crevice and disappearing into a new den. Disaster diverted. I celebrated myself; I had refused to just let go. Realistic optimism.

The snake was gone but I was still stranded. The anxiety was still pooling in the pit of my stomach but somehow, I remained calm and was able to breathe. I sat back behind the wheel, which provided some sort of comfort while I cleared my head. I resolved to walk to the nearest phone that I could find and rely on the kindness of strangers, when I suddenly had an idea. Last week, Frank had taken the Ford for a ride to the store to pick up some supplies like I'd asked him to. I still had some of the bigger stuff in the back of the truck. You know how I hate to unpack! I made my way round to the back of the vehicle and began an anxious search. Behind the supplies, I found a battered jerry can. My luck had turned.

I dragged it towards me. It was worth a try. I cautiously opened it and sniffed. It still contained some gasoline which I could hear sloshing around; not much – but hopefully enough! I eagerly hauled the can out of the back and carefully fed its contents into the tank. When I turned the ignition, initially it was a worrying sound. But I tried a few more times and then it worked. The truck choked and backfired a bit but as I pushed down on the gas pedal, the engine caught and miraculously it was ready to drive. Chug, chug, chug. What a beautiful sound!

It was not a smooth journey home but then neither had been the events of the day. It was a relief to make it home to the ranch. When I got the truck back in the garage, I went inside and called Frank. I briefly explained what happened, and he came over to help me out.

'How on earth did you manage this one?' he said as he poured me some coffee.

I thought about how to respond to his question, but I could not think of an appropriate response. We sat in silence for a while at my kitchen table when I realized that today had not been my Fin Del Mundo and tomorrow would be another day.

'I should re-name my ranch after all: the *edge* of the world, but not the end. *Borde Del Mundo,* not *Fin Del Mundo.*'

'Are you getting the paint, or shall I?' he replied.

ACKNOWLEDGEMENTS

This book is dedicated to my parents. I am eternally grateful for you. Thank you for everything: for the countless opportunities to grow and learn and fail; for your unwavering support in all of our endeavours; for always listening. But, importantly, thank you for introducing me to a whole world of different stories from a young age and still celebrating them with me today.

I am particularly indebted to my Dad for this particular collection because of his endless time and support in reading early, sketchy drafts. He was willing to read draft after draft and many of his ideas have made it into the final versions of these stories. Thank you for sharing your joy for creative writing with me.

Thank you to Ben for being my best friend and my constant in all of the chaos. Thank you for supporting me in all of my projects and believing the best in me every day. I love you.

A big thanks to my wider family, friends and colleagues who have cheered me on throughout the whole journey. It is a real joy to do life alongside you all.

Finally, a special thank you needs to go to talented and skilled friends who have not only been a great support, but who have so kindly offered their skills to help me bring this collection to life. Thanks to Kay MacLeod for being so generous with all your writerly wisdom when I had so many questions; to Laura North, for being an honest encourager and for setting goals to keep me motivated; to Michelle Barnett for sharing your creative talent to create my cover design. I love it, thank you.

Finally, thank you to all of my readers. I hope you have enjoyed reading these stories as much as I have enjoyed writing them.

ABOUT THE AUTHOR

Kelly Punton is a writer and an English teacher in the East Midlands. She reads and writes stories, plays, and poetry. Originally from Lincoln, Kelly now lives with her husband in a small town in Nottinghamshire.

*

Kelly enjoys being playful with form and language, and especially enjoys writing in magical realism and speculative fiction genres. She is fascinated by how both the extraordinary and the ordinary are essential to the human experience.

*

When Strange Calls You Home is her first collection of short stories. Her short play *Ours/Yours* was performed and produced across the East Midlands with New Perspectives Theatre Company (as part of the Emerging Perspectives Programme).

*

You can find more information by visiting her website and blog (www.kpunton.co.uk) or follow @kpuntonbooks on Instagram and Twitter or find 'Kelly Punton' on Facebook.

Printed in Great Britain
by Amazon